Sunrise Years

# OrangeBooks Publication

1st Floor, Rajhans Arcade, Mall Road, Kohka, Bhilai, Chhattisgarh 490020

Website: **www.orangebooks.in**

---

**© Copyright, 2024, Author**

All rights reserved. No part of this book may be reproduced, stored in a retrieval system, or transmitted, in any form by any means, electronic, mechanical, magnetic, optical, chemical, manual, photocopying, recording or otherwise, without the prior written consent of its writer.

**First Edition, 2024**

**ISBN:** 978-93-6554-389-6

# SUNRISE YEARS

A Comprehensive Look at Senior Care in the South Indian Context

Ashwin Kumar Iyer

**OrangeBooks Publication**
www.orangebooks.in

*Dedicated to the Loving Memory of My Father*

*Shri. R. Subramanian*

# Table of Contents

## The Aging Process and Cultural Context .........................................1

Understanding Aging: Physical and Psychological Aspects.........2

Cultural Context of Aging in South Indian Families ..................18

Role of Elders in Traditional South Indian Families....................27

Changing Family Dynamics in Urban South India .....................35

Gender and Aging: The Experience of Elderly Women ............43

## Health and Well-Being ..................................................................52

Physical Health Concerns of the Elderly ....................................53

Mental Health and Aging............................................................63

Nutritional Needs of the Elderly.................................................73

Physical Fitness and Mobility for the Elderly.............................81

Access to Healthcare and Geriatric Services .............................90

## Social and Emotional Well-Being.................................................100

Loneliness and Social Isolation in Urban Settings....................101

Family Caregiving: Challenges and Responsibilities ................111

Intergenerational Relationships in South Indian Families ......122

The Role of Faith & Spirituality in Aging ..................................133

Cultural Practices and Rituals Surrounding Aging and Death.142

**Financial and Legal Aspects** ....................................................... 151

Financial Planning for the Elderly in South Indian Context .... 152

Elderly and Property Rights in South Indian Families ............. 165

Government Policies and Schemes for the Elderly ................. 175

Legal Challenges: Elder Abuse, Rights, and Protection ........... 184

**Senior Living and Care Options** ................................................ 197

Living Arrangements: At Home vs. Senior
Living Communities ............................................................... 198

Home Care vs. Professional Care: Making the Right Choice ... 211

Technology and Aging: Innovations for Senior Care ............... 224

Planning for the Future: End-of-Life Care and Decisions ........ 235

**Future of Elder Care in South India** .......................................... 246

The Future of Elderly Care in Urban South India .................... 247

**Afterword** ............................................................................... 255

# Foreword

## Padma Shri **Dr. V. S. Natarajan**
*Senior Geriatric Physician, Educationist and Author*

*In the South Indian context, ageing is both a deeply personal and collective experience, shaped by a culture that has long revered its elders while also navigating the changes brought by modernization. Sunrise Years offers a timely and compassionate exploration of senior care, viewed through the unique lens of Indian values, traditions, and the realities of a changing society.*

*The authors guide the reader through a wide range of topics, from the deep-seated cultural practices that honour elders to the practical aspects of modern eldercare—such as financial planning, property rights, and government policies. They thoughtfully address the emotional and psychological facets of ageing, emphasising the crucial role of spirituality, family bonds, and mental well-being in the lives of seniors.*

*What makes Sunrise Years truly compelling is its seamless blend of research and humanity. It combines robust data with the real-life experiences of Indian elders, creating a vivid and complete portrayal of ageing in this unique cultural setting. This dual approach not only informs but also touches the reader, urging a reconsideration of what it means to care for our elderly.*

*For families, caregivers, and policymakers alike, Sunrise Years provides a comprehensive guide to navigating the challenges of eldercare with dignity, respect, and compassion. It invites us to participate in a broader dialogue about ageing, one that goes beyond numbers and policies to embrace the essence of what connects us as humans: our relationships, our stories, and our collective journey through life.*

*This book stands as a tribute to the elders and to the strength of familial and cultural bonds. May it inspire us all to honour, uplift, and support the elderly, ensuring that their "sunrise years" are as bright and rewarding as the years that came before.*

# Preface

In a world where cultures and lifestyles are evolving at a rapid pace, the experience of aging in India presents a unique blend of challenges, traditions, and emerging opportunities. The significance of caring for our elderly, both as individuals and as communities, is deeply embedded in the fabric of Indian society. However, the shift toward urbanization and changing family structures has created an urgent need to re-examine and adapt our approach to elder care in ways that honour tradition while embracing the future.

In *SUNRISE YEARS - A Comprehensive Look at Senior Care in the South Indian Context*, I attempt to explore the multifaceted landscape of elder care within South Indian urban families, bringing to light the distinctive blend of cultural, familial, and modern-day factors that shape this experience. My professional journey in the Senior Care Industry has given me the privilege of overseeing senior living projects and operations across several domains and I have been fortunate to witness firsthand the evolution of Senior Care in the country and myriad concerns that accompany elder care—each unique, yet unified in a shared desire for compassion and dignity. Through this book, I aim to provide readers with insights and practical approaches to caregiving and senior support, covering aspects ranging from the challenges and responsibilities of family caregiving to the crucial role of faith, spirituality, and cultural rituals in the lives of the elderly. Topics such as financial planning, property rights, government schemes, and the influence of technology in senior care are given significant focus, especially as they relate to a South Indian context.

Writing this book has been both a personal and professional journey—a reflection on my work with senior living projects and an exploration of the profound needs of the elderly community within Indian families. I hope that *SUNRISE YEARS* serves as a guide, a source of reflection, and a catalyst for compassionate care that empowers families and caregivers to make informed decisions. As we look toward the future, I am hopeful that we will embrace a new paradigm of elder care that is as resilient and enduring as the sunrise—nurturing, respectful, and full of promise.

**Ashwin Kumar Iyer**

◆◆◆

# Part 1
# The Aging Process and Cultural Context

# Understanding Aging: Physical and Psychological Aspects

Aging is an inevitable and universal process that affects every individual. It is a gradual process that begins at birth and continues throughout life, but it becomes more noticeable as we reach later stages of life. In the context of physical and psychological changes, aging manifests in a variety of ways, impacting not only the body but also the mind. While the aging process is natural, its experience can vary significantly depending on genetic, lifestyle, environmental, and social factors. Understanding these changes can help individuals and families better prepare for the challenges and opportunities that aging presents.

**Physical Aspects of Aging**

The physical aging process is marked by a decline in the body's ability to repair itself and maintain optimal function. The effects of aging on the body can be seen in nearly every system, from the skin to the bones, muscles, organs, and sensory systems. While some changes are a natural part of growing older, others may be exacerbated by lifestyle choices or chronic conditions.

**Skin and Hair Changes**

One of the most visible signs of aging is the change in the skin. As people age, the skin becomes thinner, less elastic, and more prone to wrinkles and sagging. Collagen production, which keeps the skin firm, decreases with age, leading to the formation of fine lines and deep wrinkles. Additionally, the skin's ability to retain moisture declines, causing dryness and an increased susceptibility to damage. Age spots and pigmentation changes may also occur due to long-term sun exposure.

Hair changes are another prominent marker of aging. Hair often becomes thinner and loses its pigmentation, leading to greying. The scalp may produce less oil, resulting in drier, more brittle hair. Hair loss can also be a concern for both men and women as they age, with patterns of balding or thinning becoming more pronounced.

**Musculoskeletal System: Bones and Muscles**

The bones and muscles undergo significant changes with aging. Bone density gradually decreases after the age of 30, making bones more fragile and susceptible to fractures. This is particularly concerning for women post-menopause, as the decrease in estrogen levels accelerates bone loss, leading to conditions such as osteoporosis. Osteoporosis is characterized by weakened bones and an increased risk of fractures, particularly in the hip, spine, and wrists.

The muscles also undergo a process of gradual decline, known as sarcopenia, which leads to a loss of muscle mass and strength. By the age of 70, an individual may have lost up to 30% of their muscle mass, impacting their ability to perform everyday activities such as walking, lifting, or climbing stairs. This loss of muscle strength can lead to a higher risk of falls, which in turn may result in fractures and other injuries.

Joint health also declines with age, leading to conditions like osteoarthritis, where the cartilage in the joints wears down, causing pain, stiffness, and reduced mobility. These musculoskeletal changes can significantly impact an individual's quality of life, making it harder to stay active and independent.

**Cardiovascular System**

The cardiovascular system undergoes many changes as people age. The heart's ability to pump blood efficiently decreases, and the walls of the blood vessels become thicker and less flexible, leading to higher blood pressure. This condition, known as hypertension, is common in older adults and increases the risk of heart disease, stroke, and other cardiovascular problems.

Aging also affects the heart's electrical system, leading to a higher likelihood of arrhythmias, or irregular heartbeats. Cholesterol levels tend to rise, and fatty deposits can build up in the arteries, contributing to atherosclerosis, a condition in which the arteries harden and narrow. This can restrict blood flow to vital organs, increasing the risk of heart attacks and strokes.

While some age-related cardiovascular changes are inevitable, they can be mitigated by a healthy lifestyle that includes regular physical activity, a balanced diet, and avoiding smoking and excessive alcohol consumption.

**Respiratory System**

The respiratory system also undergoes age-related changes. The lungs lose their elasticity, and the muscles involved in breathing weaken, making it more difficult to breathe deeply. This decline in lung function can reduce the body's oxygen supply, leading to fatigue and shortness of breath, especially during physical exertion. Older adults may also be more susceptible to respiratory infections such as pneumonia and bronchitis.

Conditions such as chronic obstructive pulmonary disease (COPD) and asthma can worsen with age, further affecting an individual's ability to breathe comfortably. Maintaining good respiratory health through regular exercise, avoiding smoking, and managing chronic conditions is essential for promoting lung function in old age.

**Sensory Systems: Vision, Hearing, and Taste**

The senses play a crucial role in how individuals experience the world, and aging can significantly impact these systems. Vision and hearing, in particular, are commonly affected as people age.

- **Vision:** As people age, they are more likely to develop conditions such as presbyopia, where the eye's lens loses its ability to focus on close objects. Cataracts, where the lens becomes cloudy, are also common, along with age-related macular degeneration (AMD), which affects central vision. These changes can make it difficult to perform everyday tasks such as reading or driving.

- **Hearing:** Age-related hearing loss, or presbycusis, is another common issue. It typically affects the ability to hear high-pitched sounds and can make conversations difficult to follow, especially in noisy environments. This can lead to social isolation and communication difficulties.

- **Taste and Smell:** The sense of taste and smell may also decline with age, leading to a reduced ability to enjoy food or detect dangerous smells, such as smoke or spoiled food. This decline can affect appetite and nutrition, leading to unintended weight loss or malnutrition.

### Digestive System and Metabolism

The digestive system slows down with age, leading to a range of potential issues such as constipation, indigestion, and slower absorption of nutrients. The metabolism also slows down, meaning that older adults burn fewer calories at rest than younger individuals. This can lead to weight gain if dietary habits remain unchanged. Age-related changes in the digestive system can also affect the body's ability to process and absorb essential nutrients such as calcium, vitamin D, and B vitamins. Maintaining a healthy diet rich in fiber, vitamins, and minerals, along with regular physical activity, is essential for digestive health in old age.

### Psychological Aspects of Aging

While the physical changes of aging are more visible, the psychological aspects are equally significant. Aging can affect cognitive function, emotional well-being, and social connections, all of which contribute to an individual's overall mental health and quality of life.

**Cognitive Decline**

Cognitive decline is one of the most well-known aspects of aging, and it can range from mild forgetfulness to severe impairment, as seen in conditions like Alzheimer's disease and other forms of dementia. As people age, they may experience changes in memory, processing speed, and problem-solving abilities. It is common for older adults to have difficulty recalling names or recent events, but this mild cognitive impairment does not necessarily interfere with daily life. However, more severe cognitive decline, such as dementia, can significantly impact an individual's ability to live independently. Dementia is a progressive condition that affects memory, language, reasoning, and decision-making. Alzheimer's disease is the most common form of dementia and is characterized by the accumulation of plaques and tangles in the brain, leading to brain cell death.

While cognitive decline is not inevitable, it can be influenced by lifestyle factors such as regular mental stimulation, physical activity, and a healthy diet. Engaging in activities that challenge the brain, such as reading, puzzles, or learning new skills, may help preserve cognitive function in old age.

**Emotional and Mental Health**

Aging can also have a profound effect on emotional well-being. Many older adults experience significant life changes, such as retirement, the loss of loved ones, or a decline in physical abilities, which can lead to feelings of sadness, loneliness, or anxiety. Depression is common among the elderly but is often underdiagnosed or mistaken for normal aging.

Social isolation can contribute to emotional difficulties, especially in urban environments where traditional family structures are changing. Many older adults may find themselves living alone or separated from their children and grandchildren, which can increase the risk of loneliness and depression.

However, aging can also bring positive emotional changes. Many older adults report feeling more content and emotionally stable than they did in their younger years. They may develop a greater sense of perspective, acceptance, and resilience in dealing with life's challenges. Emotional well-being in old age is closely tied to maintaining social connections, engaging in meaningful activities, and having a sense of purpose.

## Identity and Self-Perception

Aging can lead to changes in how individuals perceive themselves and their roles in society. As people retire and transition out of the workforce, they may struggle with a loss of identity or a sense of purpose. This shift can be particularly challenging in cultures that place a high value on productivity and achievement.

However, many older adults find new ways to define themselves outside of their professional roles. They may take on new hobbies, volunteer work, or caregiving responsibilities, which can provide a sense of fulfilment and purpose.

Self-perception in old age is also influenced by societal attitudes toward aging. In many cultures, including India, elders are traditionally revered and respected for their wisdom and experience. However, in modern urban societies, where youth and productivity are often celebrated, older adults may feel marginalized or undervalued.

The aging process encompasses a wide range of physical and psychological changes that impact individuals in complex ways. While physical aging is marked by changes in skin, muscles, bones, and sensory systems, psychological aging affects cognitive function, emotional well-being, and self-perception. These changes, though challenging, can be managed and mitigated through a combination of lifestyle choices, social support, and access to healthcare.

**Sociological Aspects of Aging**

Aging is not just a biological or psychological process; it is deeply embedded in the social fabric of society. The sociological aspects of aging focus on how social structures, institutions, and cultural values shape the experience of growing older. It explores how aging individuals interact with their families, communities, and the broader society, and how these interactions are influenced by factors such as socioeconomic status, gender, and cultural norms.

In many ways, the sociological aspects of aging reveal both the challenges and opportunities that older adults face as they transition into later life stages. These challenges include issues such as social isolation, ageism, and changing family dynamics, while opportunities might involve greater respect and wisdom that come with age, or evolving roles within families and communities. Understanding these dynamics is crucial for promoting a more inclusive and supportive environment for older adults, particularly in urban settings such as the cities.

**The Role of Family in Aging**

The family has historically been the primary source of support for older adults, particularly in South Asian societies where joint family systems have been the norm. In traditional Indian families, elders were considered the pillars of wisdom and authority, and they played a significant role in decision-making and maintaining family values. The younger generations were expected to care for their aging parents, offering emotional, physical, and financial support.

However, with urbanization, modernization, and the shift toward nuclear family structures, the role of the family in caring for the elderly is changing. In urban areas, younger family members are often preoccupied with demanding careers, and many live separately from their parents. This geographical and emotional distance can affect the quality of care that older adults receive from their children. As a result, many elderly people in urban India experience loneliness and a sense of abandonment, which can affect their mental and emotional well-being.

In contrast, some families still maintain strong intergenerational bonds despite these changes. Elderly parents may live with their children or in close proximity, ensuring a sense of familial connection. Moreover, as traditional caregiving models evolve, many families are opting for professional home care services or assisted living facilities to provide the necessary support to their aging members.

**Social Roles and Identity in Aging**

As people age, they experience changes in their social roles and identities. In earlier life stages, individuals may define themselves through their careers, roles as parents, or other societal positions. Retirement, the departure of children from the home (empty nest), and physical decline can alter these roles, leading to questions about purpose and self-identity.

Retirement, in particular, is a significant sociological milestone in the aging process. For many, it signals the end of their productive work life, which can be both liberating and disorienting. In cultures that place a high value on productivity and economic contribution, retired individuals may struggle with feelings of redundancy or loss of status. This challenge is heightened in societies where older adults are seen as a burden rather than contributors.

In contrast, many older adults find new roles and opportunities in retirement. Some engage in volunteer work, community service, or take on the role of caregivers for grandchildren. These roles can provide a renewed sense of purpose and social engagement, helping older adults maintain a strong sense of identity and relevance in society. In India, for instance, elders often play a significant role in guiding younger family members, participating in religious or cultural activities, and offering wisdom based on life experience.

**Social Isolation and Loneliness**

One of the most significant sociological issues associated with aging is social isolation. As people age, their social networks tend to shrink due to retirement, the death of friends or a spouse, and physical or cognitive decline that may limit mobility. This reduction in social interaction can lead to feelings of loneliness and disconnection, which are linked to negative health outcomes, such as depression, anxiety, and even premature death.

In urban India, where families are increasingly adopting a nuclear structure, older adults may find themselves living alone or without regular contact with their children. This can exacerbate feelings of loneliness, particularly for those who are not tech-savvy or able to engage with others through modern communication methods such as social media or video calls. Furthermore, mobility issues or lack of accessible public spaces for the elderly can prevent older adults from engaging in community life, further contributing to social isolation.

Community centres, senior clubs, and religious gatherings can serve as important social outlets for older adults. These settings provide opportunities for socialization, engagement, and support, helping to mitigate the effects of isolation. In South India, religious festivals, temple gatherings, and neighbourhood associations can be particularly important for elderly individuals seeking social connections. However, as society continues to urbanize, there is a need to create more age-friendly public spaces and social services that cater specifically to the elderly.

## Ageism and Societal Attitudes Toward Aging

Ageism, or discrimination based on a person's age, is a pervasive issue in many societies. Negative stereotypes about aging, such as the belief that older adults are frail, forgetful, or resistant to change, can lead to prejudice and exclusion. Ageism can manifest in the workplace, healthcare settings, and everyday interactions, affecting an older person's self-esteem and access to opportunities.

In the workplace, older adults may face pressure to retire early or may be overlooked for promotions and other opportunities due to assumptions about their abilities. This can contribute to feelings of worthlessness and loss of identity. In healthcare, ageism may lead to inadequate treatment, as medical professionals may dismiss certain symptoms as "just part of aging" rather than treating them as legitimate health concerns.

Societal attitudes toward aging can also influence public policy and the availability of resources for older adults. For instance, if a society views older adults as a burden rather than a valuable demographic, there may be fewer investments in elder care services, pension schemes, or age-friendly infrastructure.

In India, traditional respect for elders is still present in many families, but it is being challenged by modernization and Western influences that tend to emphasize youth and individualism. As societal values shift, there is a need for awareness campaigns and policy changes that challenge ageist attitudes and promote a more inclusive approach to aging.

**The Impact of Socioeconomic Status on Aging**

Socioeconomic status plays a crucial role in determining the quality of life in old age. Wealthier individuals tend to have better access to healthcare, housing, and social support, which can improve their overall well-being. Conversely, those from lower socioeconomic backgrounds may face significant challenges in accessing the resources necessary for healthy aging.

In urban societies, the economic disparity between different social classes can have a profound impact on the experience of aging. While affluent families may be able to afford high-quality healthcare, home care services, or private retirement homes, individuals from lower-income families may rely on overstretched public services or familial support that may not always be available.

The rising cost of healthcare and living in urban areas can further exacerbate financial strain, leaving many elderly people vulnerable to poverty and poor health.

Government programs, such as pension schemes and social security benefits, play a critical role in supporting older adults, but these are often insufficient to meet the needs of all elderly citizens.

Inadequate financial planning for retirement, combined with increasing life expectancy, can lead to economic insecurity for many older adults.

## Gender and Aging

Gender is another important factor in the sociological experience of aging. In many societies, women tend to live longer than men, which means they are more likely to experience the challenges of old age, including widowhood, financial insecurity, and social isolation. Additionally, women are often the primary caregivers for both children and aging relatives, which can affect their financial independence and health as they age.

Widowhood can be a particularly isolating experience for women in Indian society, where traditional gender roles often place women in a dependent position. After the death of a spouse, older women may face financial hardship, social exclusion, and a lack of support. While there has been progress in terms of women's rights and economic participation, older women may still face cultural and economic barriers that limit their access to resources.

Men, on the other hand, may struggle with loss of identity after retirement, especially if their sense of self was closely tied to their professional roles. They may also face health issues related to cardiovascular diseases or lifestyle factors and may find it difficult to seek help due to traditional ideas of masculinity that discourage vulnerability.

## Government Policies and Support for Aging Populations

In response to the growing elderly population, governments are increasingly focused on policies and programs that address the needs of older adults. In India, the National Policy on Older Persons aims to promote the welfare of the elderly by ensuring access to healthcare, social security, and age-friendly infrastructure. Programs such as the Indira Gandhi National Old Age Pension Scheme provide financial assistance to elderly individuals below the poverty line, while initiatives like the Maintenance and Welfare of Parents and Senior Citizens Act mandate that children provide financial support to their aging parents.

Despite these efforts, gaps remain in the implementation and reach of these programs. Many elderly individuals are unaware of the benefits available to them or may face bureaucratic hurdles in accessing these resources. Moreover, the quality of public healthcare for the elderly often varies, with urban centres generally offering better services than rural areas. The sociological aspects of aging encompass a wide range of factors, including family dynamics, social roles, isolation, ageism, socioeconomic status, and gender. As society continues to evolve, particularly in urban areas, the experience of aging is changing. While traditional values of respect for elders remain, they are being challenged by modernization, changing family structures, and evolving social attitudes.

Addressing the sociological aspects of aging requires a multi-faceted approach that includes supportive family structures, community engagement, government policies, and societal shifts in how aging and the elderly are viewed. By understanding and addressing these issues, society can better support older adults in maintaining their dignity, independence, and quality of life as they age.

---

**Example 1**: Rajan, a 72-year-old retired schoolteacher, notices his daily energy levels declining, making it harder to maintain his vegetable garden, a hobby he's enjoyed for decades. Physically, his joints ache, and he finds it difficult to manage tasks that once seemed simple, like kneeling or standing for extended periods. Psychologically, he finds himself reflecting more on past accomplishments and relationships. Some days, he feels pride in his achievements and close family bonds, while on other days, he experiences loneliness, missing his late wife. Rajan realizes that both physical decline and psychological introspection are natural parts of aging, and he actively seeks to stay mentally engaged by tutoring neighbourhood kids, which brings him joy and a renewed sense of purpose.

**Example 2**: Gopal, a 70 year-old retired bank officer, notices how his physical stamina has declined since his youth. A decade ago, he could climb the steep hill to the temple every morning. Now, he feels winded just climbing a few stairs. Psychologically, he struggles with the change, feeling frustrated by his limitations. To manage, Gopal joins a group of elderly friends for gentle morning walks, and they share stories and reminisce about old times. These interactions help him cope with his physical changes and give him a sense of camaraderie, making aging less daunting

# Cultural Context of Aging in South Indian Families

In Indian culture, aging and the elderly are traditionally viewed with great respect and reverence. The concept of aging is not merely a biological progression but is deeply embedded in the cultural, spiritual, and social fabric of society. The elderly, often seen as custodians of wisdom, experience, and tradition, occupy an essential place within families and communities. However, with modernization, urbanization, and changes in family structures, the cultural context of aging in South Indian families is evolving. Despite these changes, many aspects of traditional South Indian values related to aging continue to influence how families care for and relate to their elderly members.

**The Traditional Respect for Elders**

In Indian society, the elderly have historically been regarded as pillars of wisdom and authority within families. They are seen as sources of knowledge, both spiritual and practical, and are often entrusted with the role of guiding younger generations. In the hierarchical family structure typical of India, elders were accorded a prominent status, their opinions valued in decision-making processes. They played a key role in maintaining family traditions, overseeing religious rituals, and ensuring the transmission of cultural values to the next generation.

This respect for elders is rooted in the principles of **Dharma** (duty) as outlined in Hindu philosophy, which emphasizes the duty of younger family members to care for and honour their parents and grandparents. The **Vedas** and **Puranas**, ancient Indian texts, uphold the principle of **Matru Devo Bhava, Pitru Devo Bhava**—"Mother is God, Father is God"—signifying the divine status attributed to parents and elders. Traditionally, the elder members of the family have been viewed as embodiments of patience, virtue, and piety.

**The Role of Elders in Family and Society**

In the traditional joint family system, which was once the norm, the elderly played a central role in the family. They were not only respected for their age and wisdom but were also crucial in decision-making processes, particularly in matters related to property, marriage, and family disputes. Elders acted as moral and spiritual guides, overseeing rituals, religious observances, and the education of grandchildren in religious and cultural practices.

In many Indian households, grandparents continue to play a significant role in child-rearing. The joint family system allowed for strong intergenerational bonds, where the elderly provided childcare while parents focused on earning a living. This arrangement fostered a sense of belonging, continuity, and shared responsibility within the family. For the elderly, these roles provided a sense of purpose and emotional fulfilment, as they remained active contributors to the family's well-being.

**Spirituality and the Aging Process**

In Indian culture, aging is often viewed through a spiritual lens. As individuals grow older, they are expected to focus more on spiritual pursuits, gradually withdrawing from the material world. This stage of life, known as **Vanaprastha** in Hinduism, is traditionally marked by a reduction in worldly responsibilities and an increasing focus on religious and spiritual activities. Elders often spend more time engaging in prayer, meditation, temple visits, and rituals, passing on religious teachings to the younger generation.

Many elderly individuals Indian families are seen as spiritual guides, taking on the responsibility of conducting household rituals and ceremonies. Their knowledge of religious texts, mantras, and customs is invaluable, and they often lead significant family ceremonies such as weddings, naming rituals, and death rites.

Additionally, religious festivals play an important role in maintaining social and cultural ties among the elderly. In South India, festivals such as **Pongal** in Tamil Nadu, **Ugadi** in Karnataka and Andhra Pradesh, and **Onam** in Kerala are occasions where elders are honoured, and their blessings are sought for prosperity and well-being. These festivals provide opportunities for intergenerational bonding and reaffirm the cultural and spiritual significance of the elderly in society.

**The Changing Family Structure: From Joint to Nuclear Families**

One of the most significant changes in the cultural context of aging has been the shift from joint family structures to nuclear families.

Urbanization, industrialization, and migration for education and employment have contributed to this transition. In the traditional joint family system, multiple generations lived under one roof, and caring for the elderly was seen as a shared responsibility among family members.

However, as more young adults move to cities for work and pursue independent nuclear family lives, the care of elderly parents has become more challenging. Many older adults are left to live alone or in old age homes, which were once rare in Indian society but are now becoming more common in urban areas. The shift from joint to nuclear families has led to a reduction in the day-to-day interaction between generations, potentially contributing to feelings of loneliness and isolation among the elderly.

Despite this shift, the cultural expectation that children will care for their aging parents remains strong. In many cases, even when living separately, families maintain close ties, with children regularly visiting or financially supporting their elderly parents. However, the modern nuclear family often grapples with balancing work, caregiving responsibilities, and the pressures of urban living, leading to new challenges in eldercare.

## Eldercare in Modern South Indian Society

Traditionally, caring for the elderly in Indian families was seen as a duty and a form of **Seva** (selfless service), deeply embedded in cultural and religious practices. However, as life expectancy increases and families become more dispersed, the nature of eldercare is changing. While many families still uphold the cultural norm of caring for their elderly members, practical challenges such as the pressures of work, lack of time, and geographical distance have led to a growing reliance on alternative forms of care.

Urban families are increasingly turning to professional caregiving services, home healthcare providers, and assisted living facilities to meet the needs of their aging relatives. This shift reflects changing attitudes toward eldercare, where professional help is no longer seen as a failure of family responsibility but as a necessary and practical solution to meet the complex needs of aging parents.

Old age homes, once a culturally taboo concept in South India, are becoming more accepted in urban areas. However, for many families, sending an elderly parent to an old age home still carries a sense of guilt or shame, as it may be perceived as neglecting one's duty. Nonetheless, as family structures evolve and as life in urban environments becomes more demanding, old age homes are seen as viable options, especially for elderly individuals who require medical attention or who do not have family members capable of providing full-time care.

## The Role of Women in Eldercare

In Indian families, women have traditionally borne the primary responsibility for caring for elderly relatives. This caregiving role is often seen as part of their duty as daughters or daughters-in-law, and it is deeply ingrained in cultural expectations. Women are expected to provide emotional support, manage the household, and attend to the daily needs of elderly family members, even while balancing their own careers and responsibilities.

However, the changing role of women in society—particularly in urban areas, where women are increasingly part of the workforce—has led to a shift in how caregiving responsibilities are managed. While women continue to play a crucial role in eldercare, there is growing recognition that caregiving must be a shared responsibility within the family. Professional caregiving services are often sought to alleviate the burden on female family members, allowing them to balance their careers with their familial obligations.

**Cultural Tensions: Tradition vs. Modernity**

As society modernizes, cultural tensions between traditional values and modern lifestyles are becoming more pronounced, particularly in the context of aging and eldercare. On one hand, the cultural expectation to respect and care for the elderly remains strong, deeply rooted in religious and familial traditions. On the other hand, the realities of urban life—long work hours, smaller living spaces, and the geographical dispersion of families—have made it more difficult for younger generations to fulfil these responsibilities in the same way their ancestors did.

This tension is particularly evident in the way families approach decisions about eldercare. While many urban families continue to provide in-home care for their aging relatives, others are turning to professional caregiving services or old age homes, sometimes causing friction between the generations. For the elderly, adjusting to these modern arrangements can be challenging, as they may feel a sense of abandonment or loss of purpose.

## Social Status and the Elderly in South India

In South Indian culture, an individual's social status is often closely tied to their role within the family and community. For the elderly, maintaining their status as respected and valued members of the family is crucial to their sense of identity and self-worth. However, the shift toward modern, individualistic lifestyles has led to a redefinition of status in many urban families.

In traditional settings, the elderly were often revered for their wisdom and experience, particularly in rural areas where family and community ties remain strong. In urban areas, however, the fast-paced, competitive environment may lead to older individuals feeling sidelined or less valued. Despite this, many elderly Indians continue to command respect within their families, particularly during religious and cultural ceremonies, where their role as knowledge bearers is still honoured.

## Intergenerational Relationships and Conflict

In Indian families, intergenerational relationships are often close-knit, with a strong emphasis on respect for elders. However, as younger generations adopt more modern, individualistic lifestyles, conflicts may arise. The expectations of the elderly, shaped by traditional values, may clash with the aspirations and lifestyles of their children or grandchildren.

For example, issues such as career choices, marriage, and lifestyle decisions may become points of contention. Elders may expect their children to adhere to traditional norms, while younger generations may seek more autonomy and freedom in their choices. These intergenerational conflicts, though not unique to Indian families, are often heightened by the rapid pace of cultural change in urban settings.

Despite these challenges, many families maintain strong intergenerational bonds. The practice of seeking blessings from elders, especially during festivals, important family events, and life milestones, is still common. The emotional and spiritual connection between generations remains a significant aspect of family life.

The cultural context of aging in families is deeply rooted in traditions of respect, duty, and spiritual engagement. Elders have historically played a central role in family life, contributing wisdom, guidance, and cultural continuity. However, as the country urbanizes and family structures shift from joint to nuclear arrangements, the experience of aging is changing. While the traditional values of caring for the elderly remain strong, practical realities have led to the emergence of new forms of eldercare, including professional caregiving services and old age homes.

Despite these changes, the core cultural values that emphasize respect for elders and the importance of intergenerational relationships continue to shape how families approach aging. As society continues to evolve, there is a need for a balanced approach that honours cultural traditions while adapting to the demands of modern urban life, ensuring that the elderly continue to be valued and cared for in meaningful ways.

**Example 1**: Meenakshi, an 80-year-old matriarch, lives with her extended family in Chennai. Her children and grandchildren regard her as the family's cultural anchor, turning to her for advice on traditional practices, festival rituals, and family history. Every Diwali, she oversees the making of sweets and the lighting of oil lamps, sharing stories of her own childhood Diwalis in a small Tamil Nadu village. Meenakshi's presence ensures that traditions remain strong within her family, as they gather each year to listen to her guidance and celebrate customs passed down for generations. Her role as a custodian of cultural values exemplifies the view of elders as vital carriers of tradition.

**Example 2**: Parvati, a respected elder in her village, is known for her knowledge of traditional herbal remedies. During festival seasons, her children and grandchildren gather around her to learn how to make specific herbal concoctions, like turmeric-based drinks for immunity and sesame oil massages for joint pain. Parvati's knowledge is invaluable, as it keeps alive traditional practices rooted in heritage. Her family often reflects on how her wisdom keeps them connected to their roots, teaching them to value natural healing methods that have been passed down through generations.

# Role of Elders in Traditional South Indian Families

Elders have long held a revered position in traditional South Indian families, not only as the custodians of culture, wisdom, and family values but also as decision-makers who provide stability and guidance across generations. Their role transcends the mere biological relationship of age and authority; they embody the heart of familial responsibility, spiritual leadership, and social governance within the household. The unique cultural practices of, deeply rooted in family-centred values and religious customs, place great importance on the role of elders, especially within the extended joint family system, which was once the most common living arrangement in this region.

**Elders as Custodians of Tradition and Culture**

One of the central roles of elders in traditional families is their function as custodians of culture, tradition, and religious practices. India is home to a rich and diverse set of religious practices, including Hinduism, Islam, and Christianity, where rituals, prayers, and religious customs play an integral part in daily life. Elders, especially grandparents, are often the ones who pass down these practices to younger generations.

They oversee religious ceremonies, conduct family pujas (prayers), and ensure that cultural practices are maintained. Festivals such as

**Pongal** (in Tamil Nadu), **Ugadi** (in Karnataka and Andhra Pradesh), and **Onam** (in Kerala) hold special importance, with elders taking charge of the rituals and family activities associated with these events. Their participation and leadership in such events reaffirm their role as the keepers of tradition, ensuring that the cultural continuity of the family is preserved.

Elders also play a crucial role in teaching the next generation about family values, moral lessons, and stories from religious texts like the **Ramayana**, **Mahabharata**, and **Bhagavad Gita** in Hindu households, or the **Qur'an** in Muslim families. They ensure that children and grandchildren are familiar with the foundational stories and principles of their faith and cultural identity, passing on not only knowledge but also a sense of belonging and continuity.

**Moral and Spiritual Leadership**

In traditional families, elders are seen as the moral and spiritual leaders. This role stems from the belief that with age comes wisdom, and that older individuals are better equipped to guide others in matters of ethics, morality, and spirituality. Elders often serve as counsellors, advising younger family members on how to navigate life's challenges while adhering to the ethical standards set by their culture and religion.

The spiritual leadership provided by elders is closely tied to the Hindu concept of **Vanaprastha**, the third stage of life according to Hindu philosophy. In this stage, individuals are expected to retreat from material concerns and focus more on spirituality and service to others. While not all elders in Indian families formally adopt this stage, the principle of growing spiritually and imparting spiritual wisdom is prevalent. Their role in leading prayers, performing rituals, and guiding the family in times of crisis—whether spiritual or personal—cements their status as moral and spiritual anchors within the household.

**Decision-Making and Conflict Resolution**

Elders in traditional families are often the ultimate authority in decision-making processes, particularly in matters related to family welfare, finances, marriages, and property. Their life experience, combined with their understanding of family values and social norms, positions them as the ideal arbiters of family disputes and the primary decision-makers in significant family matters.

In the extended family or **joint family system**, which was once prevalent across India, multiple generations lived together under one roof, sharing responsibilities and resources. In such a system, the eldest male, often referred to as the **Karta**, acted as the head of the family. He was responsible for managing family finances, distributing wealth and property, and making important decisions regarding the welfare of the family. Even when younger generations took on more active roles in earning and running the household, major decisions typically required the approval or at least the consultation of the eldest members of the family.

Elders also play a critical role in arranging marriages, which are often seen as a family affair in Indian culture. They are involved in selecting suitable matches, ensuring that alliances are made within appropriate social, economic, and cultural circles, and that traditions like dowry negotiations (although controversial in modern times) are conducted according to customs. The involvement of elders in marriage arrangements symbolizes their role as guardians of the family's future and its relationships with the broader community.

In times of conflict within the family, whether related to property disputes, disagreements between siblings, or marital issues, elders are often looked to for mediation and resolution. Their position of respect and neutrality enables them to intervene effectively and provide solutions that prioritize family harmony and collective well-being. Their ability to resolve conflicts without allowing matters to escalate reflects the deep trust that younger family members place in their judgment.

**Caregivers and Emotional Support**

While much of the focus on the role of elders in families is on their leadership and decision-making responsibilities, their role as caregivers and emotional supporters is equally important. In traditional families, elders, particularly grandmothers, often take on a nurturing role, helping raise grandchildren and managing household duties while parents are occupied with work or other responsibilities.

The presence of elders in the home provides emotional stability and support to family members. They offer comfort during difficult times, such as the loss of a family member, and provide advice and emotional guidance during key life transitions, such as marriage, childbirth, or career challenges. In many cases, grandparents serve as confidants to their grandchildren, offering wisdom and support without the judgment that younger parents might impose.

This role as caregivers extends beyond just emotional support; it also includes practical day-to-day responsibilities. In joint families, the elder women of the household often play a significant role in cooking, managing the household, and caring for young children, ensuring that the family runs smoothly. Even in more modern nuclear family setups, the advice and guidance of elders in running the household are often sought and valued.

## Social and Community Influence

Elders in traditional families not only hold influence within their own households but also play an important role in the wider community. Their social networks, which may include extended family members, neighbours, and religious communities, allow them to wield significant social influence. For example, the opinions of elders are often sought in village or neighbourhood matters, particularly in rural South India, where community cohesion is paramount.

In many cases, elders act as intermediaries between the family and the community, representing the family's interests in social, religious, and civic activities. Their involvement in community functions, temple committees, and religious festivals further enhances their status and reinforces their role as respected figures within the broader social fabric.

Additionally, elders often act as a bridge between the traditional practices of the past and the modern realities of present-day society. Their ability to impart wisdom gained through years of experience makes them crucial players in ensuring that the cultural and moral values of the family are not lost amidst societal changes.

## Changes in the Role of Elders with Modernization

Despite the deep cultural roots of elder respect and their significant role in traditional families, modernization and urbanization have altered family structures, often diminishing the central role of elders. The joint family system has largely given way to nuclear families, particularly in urban areas, where younger generations move away from their ancestral homes for education and employment. This geographical separation limits the everyday influence of elders in decision-making and reduces their direct involvement in family life.

In modern nuclear families, while elders may still be consulted for major decisions or invited to stay during important family events, their authority over daily matters has lessened. Moreover, the increasing availability of professional caregiving services and old-age homes has changed the dynamic of eldercare, sometimes shifting the responsibility from the family to external support systems.

However, despite these changes, the cultural expectation of showing respect to elders and seeking their blessings during key life events remains strong in the society. Even in nuclear families, it is customary to involve elders in religious ceremonies, seek their approval for marriages, and celebrate festivals with their participation.

Elders have traditionally played an indispensable role in Indian families, serving as custodians of culture, spiritual leaders, decision-makers, caregivers, and sources of emotional support. Their influence within the family structure extends beyond individual households, impacting broader community relationships and social cohesion. Despite the changing social landscape, with the decline of the joint family system and the rise of nuclear families, the respect and reverence for elders remain an integral part of the cultural identity.

As modernization continues to reshape family dynamics, the challenge for the society will be to maintain the essential role of elders in family and cultural life, while adapting to the practical realities of modern urban living. Balancing traditional values with modern pressures will ensure that elders continue to be honoured and their wisdom valued in evolving family structures.

**Example**: Vishwanath, an 85-year-old grandfather, is highly respected by his family members, who look up to him for guidance on family decisions. Recently, his granddaughter was considering a job opportunity abroad. Unsure whether to encourage her to pursue her ambitions or stay close to the family, her parents sought Vishwanath's advice. He sat down with the family, reminding them of the values of unity and the significance of family connections. However, he also shared stories of how he encouraged his own children to pursue their dreams. His balanced perspective gave his granddaughter clarity, and she ultimately decided to accept the job, with the assurance that her family would support her.

**Example**: Kannan, an 82-year-old patriarch, is the go-to person for important family decisions, particularly regarding marriage alliances. Recently, his grandson expressed interest in marrying someone from a different cultural background. Kannan, while initially hesitant, took time to speak with the couple, and over a series of discussions, he came to see the depth of their bond. His acceptance brought harmony to the family, showing how his wisdom and patience allowed for a modern yet respectful approach to tradition. Kannan's role in decision-making highlights the balance elders bring to family matters, maintaining unity while adapting to change.

# Changing Family Dynamics in Urban South India

The traditional family structure in South India has historically been characterized by joint families, where multiple generations live together under one roof. However, in recent decades, urbanization, economic development, and changing social values have led to a significant shift toward nuclear families. This transition has profound implications for the elderly, affecting their living conditions, social status, and overall quality of life. Understanding these changing family dynamics is essential to addressing the needs and challenges faced by older adults in contemporary society.

**The Transition from Joint to Nuclear Families**

Historically, joint families were the norm in South India, where extended family units comprising parents, children, grandparents, uncles, aunts, and cousins lived together. This structure provided a robust support system for all family members, especially the elderly, who were cared for by younger generations. The roles and responsibilities were clearly defined, with elders often taking on leadership roles, guiding family decisions, and imparting cultural and religious values.

However, the post-independence period saw significant changes in societal norms and economic conditions. Factors contributing to the decline of the joint family system include:

**Urbanization**: Migration to cities for better job opportunities has led to the breakdown of traditional family structures. Young adults often leave their hometowns to pursue education and careers, resulting in dispersed family units.

**Economic Independence**: With more women entering the workforce and gaining financial independence, there has been a shift in familial expectations and roles. This economic independence allows younger generations to live separately from their parents.

**Changing Social Values**: The rise of individualism, influenced by globalization and exposure to Western cultures, has shifted attitudes toward family life. Many young people prioritize personal choice, career aspirations, and lifestyles over the traditional obligation to care for aging parents.

These factors have collectively contributed to a growing preference for nuclear families, where parents and their children live independently, often without the involvement of extended family members.

### Implications for the Elderly

The shift from joint to nuclear families has profound implications for the elderly in urban society:

- **Living Arrangements**: Many elderly individuals who were once integral members of joint families now find themselves living alone or with a spouse. This shift can lead to feelings of loneliness and isolation, particularly for those accustomed to the company of larger family units. The lack of daily interaction with children and grandchildren can adversely affect their mental and emotional well-being.

- **Reduced Support Systems**: In nuclear families, the caregiving responsibilities traditionally shared among extended family members often fall solely on a single child or couple. This concentrated burden can lead to stress and challenges in balancing work, family, and caregiving roles, potentially resulting in inadequate support for the elderly.

- **Financial Security**: The financial dynamics of nuclear families may differ significantly from those of joint families. In joint families, resources were pooled together, allowing for better financial security and shared responsibilities for elderly care. In nuclear setups, the financial burden of supporting aging parents may strain the household budget, particularly if there are multiple dependents. This can lead to difficult choices regarding eldercare, including the need for professional services or alternative arrangements.

- **Access to Healthcare**: Access to healthcare can become more complicated for the elderly living in nuclear families.

With younger family members often busy with work commitments, taking elderly relatives to medical appointments or managing healthcare needs can be challenging. In joint families, elder care was often a shared responsibility, ensuring that medical needs were promptly addressed.

**Social Isolation and Emotional Challenges**

The emotional and social impact of transitioning to nuclear families is particularly significant for the elderly. Social isolation can lead to various psychological issues, including:

- **Depression and Anxiety**: The lack of daily interactions with family members can contribute to feelings of loneliness and depression. Many elderly individuals may find it difficult to adapt to new living arrangements, especially if they are used to the constant presence of family.

- **Loss of Purpose**: In traditional joint families, elders often had defined roles as caregivers, mentors, and spiritual guides. In nuclear families, these roles may diminish, leading to a sense of loss of purpose and identity. This change can be particularly challenging for those who have dedicated their lives to raising children and managing family responsibilities.

- **Communication Barriers**: Modern urban lifestyles often lead to a lack of communication between generations. Younger family members may be preoccupied with work and social commitments, leaving little time for meaningful interactions with their elderly relatives. This can further exacerbate feelings of loneliness and disconnect.

**Adapting to New Realities**

Despite the challenges posed by changing family dynamics, many families in urban South India are finding ways to adapt and maintain connections with their elderly members. Some approaches include:

- **Regular Communication**: With the proliferation of technology, families are increasingly using phone calls, video chats, and social media to stay connected with their elderly relatives. Regular communication can help bridge the emotional gap and provide a sense of belonging for both generations.

- **Shared Living Arrangements**: Some families opt for multi-generational living arrangements, where parents and their adult children live in the same household or nearby. This arrangement allows for greater involvement of elders in family life while still maintaining some degree of independence.

- **Community Support**: Community initiatives, such as elder care programs, support groups, and social clubs, are becoming increasingly important in urban areas. These programs provide opportunities for elderly individuals to engage socially, participate in activities, and receive support from peers.

- **Professional Care Services**: As more families face the challenges of eldercare, the demand for professional caregiving services has increased. Home healthcare services, adult day care programs, and assisted living facilities are becoming more common, offering alternatives for families unable to provide full-time care.

## Cultural Attitudes Toward Eldercare

Despite the challenges associated with nuclear family dynamics, traditional cultural attitudes toward elder respect and care remain strong in India. Many young adults still feel a deep sense of obligation to care for their aging parents, even if they cannot do so on a daily basis. This sense of duty is often reinforced by societal expectations and the moral teachings of their upbringing.

Elders continue to be respected figures within families, and their wisdom is valued in decision-making processes, particularly concerning important family matters. Younger generations are often encouraged to seek the advice and blessings of their elders during significant life events, such as marriages, childbirth, and career changes, reflecting the enduring cultural reverence for age and experience.

The shift from joint to nuclear families in urban society represents a significant change in family dynamics, profoundly affecting the elderly population. While this transition brings challenges such as social isolation, reduced support systems, and emotional difficulties, it also presents opportunities for families to adapt and create new ways of maintaining connections with their elders.

Understanding the impact of these changing dynamics is crucial for developing effective strategies to support elderly individuals in urban settings. As Indian society continues to evolve, there is a pressing need to balance the values of tradition with the realities of modern life, ensuring that the elderly remain respected, supported, and integrated into the family and community fabric. By fostering intergenerational relationships, leveraging technology for communication, and exploring innovative care solutions, families can navigate these changes while honouring the dignity and wisdom of their elders.

> **Example 1**: Anand and Lakshmi, a middle-aged couple, live with their two children in Bengaluru. Unlike previous generations, they live in a nuclear family setting, far from their parents, who reside in a rural Tamil Nadu village. Anand recalls growing up in a bustling joint family with cousins, aunts, and uncles always around, sharing daily routines and responsibilities. In contrast, his children experience a more secluded, individual-focused lifestyle, where family interactions are limited to video calls. This shift has led Anand to ponder the challenges faced by his parents, who rely on neighbours and friends for companionship and support. He has begun considering ways to bridge this gap, such as monthly visits and encouraging his children to bond with their grandparents.

**Example 2**: Seetha, who grew up in a joint family in Kerala, now lives in a small apartment in Hyderabad with her husband and child. Her elderly mother lives back in Kerala with her brother's family. Seetha remembers the vibrant atmosphere of her childhood home, always bustling with laughter and conversation. Her own nuclear family setting feels quieter, with limited interaction among family members. She often worries about her mother's well-being and misses the closeness of her extended family. Determined to stay connected, Seetha arranges weekly video calls with her mother and even encourages her young son to learn his grandmother's favourite Malayalam rhymes to keep a sense of family continuity.

# Gender and Aging: The Experience of Elderly Women

Aging is a universal experience, yet it affects individuals in distinct ways based on gender, cultural background, and social context. In many societies, elderly women face unique challenges and experiences due to historical, economic, and social inequalities. These factors often influence their quality of life, health, social roles, and access to resources in old age. Understanding the intersection of gender and aging, especially as it relates to elderly women, reveals how traditional gender roles, economic dependence, and social isolation impact their lives, leading to a gendered experience of aging that requires specific attention and support.

**Gender and Longevity**

Globally, women tend to live longer than men. According to the World Health Organization, women have a higher life expectancy, often outliving men by an average of five to seven years. While this trend reflects advancements in healthcare and social conditions, it also leads to specific challenges for elderly women. Longer life expectancy means that women are more likely to experience physical and cognitive declines associated with aging, and they are also more likely to live alone after the death of a spouse.

Longevity has economic and social implications. Elderly women, especially those who have outlived their spouses or children, may face financial insecurity due to limited income sources or insufficient retirement funds. This economic vulnerability is further compounded for women who may not have been part of the workforce or who relied on their spouses for financial stability.

**Economic Insecurity and Dependence**

Economic insecurity is one of the most pressing challenges elderly women face worldwide. Throughout history, traditional gender roles often designated men as primary breadwinners while women took on unpaid caregiving roles. As a result, many elderly women, particularly those from older generations, may lack a formal work history or have limited access to retirement benefits and pensions. Even in cases where they have been part of the workforce, they might have experienced pay inequities, impacting their financial security in old age. For elderly women who were homemakers, the dependence on their spouse's income or family support can lead to significant financial difficulties if their partner passes away or if family relationships become strained. This economic vulnerability can leave them reliant on social services, which may be limited or difficult to access, especially for women from marginalized communities.

The intersection of age and gender can create a "feminization of poverty" in old age. Elderly women are disproportionately represented among the economically disadvantaged, facing high rates of poverty due to limited savings and assets. Without a financial safety net, these women are more vulnerable to neglect and abuse and may have limited access to healthcare and other essential services.

**Health Disparities and Access to Care**

Health disparities between men and women in old age are closely related to both biological and social factors. Elderly women are more likely to suffer from chronic conditions such as arthritis, osteoporosis, and depression, partly due to biological factors such as hormonal changes and bone density loss. They are also at higher risk of disability, limiting their mobility and independence.

Access to healthcare is crucial in managing these health conditions, but elderly women often face unique barriers in accessing adequate care. Financial constraints, lack of transportation, and limited family support can make it difficult for them to visit doctors, obtain medications, or undergo necessary procedures. In some societies, healthcare systems may also prioritize men's health or be less responsive to the specific needs of elderly women, further exacerbating these health disparities.

The mental health of elderly women is another area of concern. Depression, anxiety, and loneliness are common, especially for women who live alone or lack a strong social support system. The mental health struggles of elderly women are often linked to past experiences of caregiving and the social expectations of their role. Having been primary caregivers for much of their lives, many elderly women may feel a loss of identity and purpose once they are no longer in a caregiving role, contributing to emotional distress and a sense of isolation.

## Social Roles and Identity

Throughout their lives, women are often defined by their relationships and caregiving roles as mothers, wives, daughters, and caregivers. In old age, these social roles may shift, especially if their children have grown up and their spouses have passed away. For many elderly women, the loss of these roles can lead to a crisis of identity and a sense of purposelessness.

Elderly women, especially those who were once central figures in their families, may find it challenging to redefine their roles as they age. In cultures that prioritize youth and productivity, elderly women may feel marginalized and devalued. Without the caregiving responsibilities that defined much of their lives, some elderly women struggle with feelings of invisibility and irrelevance, which can have a profound impact on their mental health and well-being.

In societies where ageism is prevalent, elderly women may also face negative stereotypes that further erode their sense of self-worth. Ageism can lead to exclusion from social activities, diminished participation in community life, and limited representation in media and popular culture, reinforcing feelings of isolation and marginalization among elderly women.

## Social Isolation and Loneliness

Social isolation is a significant issue for elderly women, particularly those who live alone. Older women are more likely to be widowed or to live alone compared to older men, and this isolation can lead to feelings of loneliness and emotional distress. Social isolation is not only emotionally challenging but also associated with a range of negative health outcomes, including increased risks of heart disease, stroke, and cognitive decline.

Cultural shifts, particularly in urban areas, have weakened traditional family structures that once provided elderly women with a strong support system. As nuclear families become more common, elderly women may have fewer interactions with extended family members, particularly in societies where younger generations are highly mobile and frequently move away for education and employment.

While community programs and senior centres can provide valuable social opportunities for elderly women, barriers such as limited mobility, lack of transportation, and social stigma can prevent them from participating. Furthermore, societal norms and expectations may discourage elderly women from actively seeking companionship or social engagement, reinforcing feelings of isolation.

**Elder Abuse and Gender-Based Violence**

Elder abuse is a significant concern for elderly women, who may be particularly vulnerable due to physical frailty, financial dependence, or social isolation. Forms of elder abuse include physical, emotional, financial, and psychological abuse, as well as neglect and abandonment. Elderly women, especially those who live with family members or in institutional settings, may be at risk of abuse from caregivers or family members.

Gender-based violence remains a concern even in old age. Elderly women who may have experienced domestic violence earlier in life sometimes continue to face abuse in old age, particularly in settings where they are financially dependent on their abuser. In societies where elder abuse is stigmatized or not adequately addressed by legal systems, elderly women may lack the resources or support to report abuse or seek help.

**Impact of Cultural Expectations on Aging Women**

Cultural norms and expectations significantly shape the experience of aging for women. In many cultures, elderly women are expected to be caregivers, even in old age. This expectation can place a heavy burden on elderly women who may already be struggling with their health. In multigenerational households, for example, elderly women may be expected to assist in raising grandchildren or managing household tasks, despite physical limitations.

Cultural perceptions of aging women can also impact their social status. In societies where youth and beauty are highly valued, elderly women may feel pressured to conform to unrealistic standards or experience age-related shame. These cultural pressures can have profound effects on their self-esteem and mental health.

**Widowhood and Its Impact on Elderly Women**

Widowhood is a common experience for elderly women, as they are more likely to outlive their spouses. In many societies, widowhood carries social and economic consequences that affect women's well-being. Widows may face financial difficulties, especially if they relied on their husband's income or do not have access to pension benefits. Additionally, in some cultures, widowhood is stigmatized, and elderly widows may experience discrimination or exclusion from community activities.

In certain cultures, widowhood involves specific rituals and restrictions that may limit a woman's social interactions or place additional burdens on her. These cultural expectations can further isolate elderly women, impacting their social relationships and quality of life.

**Resilience and Strength of Elderly Women**

Despite the many challenges they face, elderly women often demonstrate remarkable resilience and strength. Many elderly women find meaning and purpose in spirituality, community service, and maintaining connections with family and friends. Religious practices and community gatherings provide emotional support and foster a sense of belonging, helping elderly women cope with the challenges of aging.

The adaptability of elderly women, honed over years of managing family, caregiving, and societal expectations, often becomes a source of strength in later life. Many elderly women become active participants in community initiatives, mentoring younger generations, and sharing their life experiences. These contributions highlight the importance of recognizing the strengths and resilience that elderly women bring to their families and communities.

The experience of aging for elderly women is shaped by a complex interplay of gender, economic status, cultural expectations, and social roles. Elderly women face unique challenges, from economic insecurity and health disparities to social isolation and elder abuse. These issues are compounded by traditional gender roles and societal expectations that can limit their access to resources and support. However, elderly women also possess unique resilience, adaptability, and strength, cultivated through years of caregiving, relationship-building, and community involvement.

Addressing the gendered experience of aging requires a multifaceted approach that includes social support, healthcare access, legal protections, and community engagement. Policymakers, healthcare providers, and communities must recognize the specific needs of elderly women and develop strategies that promote their well-being, dignity, and independence in old age. By creating inclusive and supportive environments, society can honour the contributions of elderly women and ensure that they age with respect, security, and a sense of belonging.

**Example 1**: Saraswathi, a 78-year-old widow, lives alone in a small town in Tamil Nadu. As a young woman, her responsibilities revolved around her family and home, supporting her husband and raising their children. Now, as her children have moved abroad, Saraswathi faces a sense of invisibility in society. Although she is still actively involved in temple activities and attends community gatherings, she often feels that her opinions carry less weight than they did when she was younger. However, with encouragement from her daughter, Saraswathi began attending a local women's group, where she shares her cooking skills and enjoys learning crafts. This shift has not only provided her with companionship but has also given her a renewed sense of identity and purpose.

**Example 2**: Kamakshi, a 79-year-old widow, spent her entire life managing household responsibilities and supporting her husband's career. Now, in her old age, she feels an increasing sense of isolation. Although her children love her deeply, they lead busy lives, and she struggles with finding a purpose. To rediscover her sense of self, Kamakshi decides to volunteer at the local temple, where she helps organize religious gatherings and meals for underprivileged children. Here, she finds companionship with other elderly women, exchanging stories, laughter, and a newfound confidence in her own worth beyond traditional roles.

# Part 2
# Health and Well-Being

# Physical Health Concerns of the Elderly

Aging is a natural process that brings about numerous physiological changes, leading to various health challenges for elderly individuals. While aging affects every system in the body, the severity and impact of these changes can vary significantly among individuals due to factors such as genetics, lifestyle, diet, and environmental conditions. Some health problems are more common among the elderly and require special attention and management to improve quality of life and longevity. This chapter explores some of the most prevalent health issues faced by older adults, including arthritis, diabetes, hypertension, and other age-related conditions, discussing their causes, symptoms, and treatment options.

**Arthritis**

Arthritis is one of the most common health concerns among the elderly, affecting joints and causing pain, swelling, and stiffness. The two main types of arthritis that affect older adults are osteoarthritis and rheumatoid arthritis.

- **Osteoarthritis**: This type of arthritis is a degenerative joint disease that occurs when the cartilage cushioning the joints breaks down, leading to pain and stiffness. It is most commonly seen in weight-bearing joints like the knees, hips, and spine. Osteoarthritis is often caused by years of joint wear and tear, obesity, and genetics. Symptoms typically include joint pain during movement, stiffness after periods of inactivity, and decreased flexibility in the affected joints. While osteoarthritis cannot be cured, treatments focus on pain relief, improving joint function, and preventing further damage. Physical therapy, lifestyle changes (like weight management), anti-inflammatory medications, and, in some cases, joint replacement surgery can help alleviate symptoms.

- **Rheumatoid Arthritis**: Unlike osteoarthritis, rheumatoid arthritis is an autoimmune disease where the body's immune system attacks the joints, causing inflammation, pain, and eventual joint damage. It can affect multiple joints and often involves systemic symptoms such as fatigue and fever. While it can occur at any age, it is more severe and challenging to manage in the elderly. Treatment typically involves medications like disease-modifying antirheumatic drugs (DMARDs), steroids, and physical therapy to manage pain and reduce inflammation.

## Diabetes

Diabetes is a chronic metabolic disorder where the body cannot effectively use insulin, leading to elevated blood sugar levels. In elderly populations, diabetes is often complicated by other age-related health conditions, requiring careful monitoring and management.

- **Type 2 Diabetes**: This is the most common form of diabetes in older adults. Age-related changes in glucose metabolism, along with lifestyle factors such as physical inactivity, poor diet, and obesity, increase the risk of developing type 2 diabetes. Symptoms include excessive thirst, frequent urination, fatigue, blurred vision, and slow-healing sores. However, in the elderly, symptoms may be subtle and often mistaken for normal signs of aging, leading to delayed diagnosis. Proper management of diabetes in elderly patients focuses on diet modification, regular physical activity, weight control, and, when necessary, medications like metformin or insulin. Regular monitoring of blood sugar levels is essential to prevent complications such as neuropathy, retinopathy, and cardiovascular diseases.

- **Complications of Diabetes in the Elderly**: Uncontrolled diabetes can lead to severe complications, particularly in older adults. Diabetic neuropathy (nerve damage) can cause numbness and pain in the extremities, while diabetic retinopathy (damage to the eyes) may lead to vision loss. Cardiovascular disease is also common among diabetic individuals. Managing these complications requires comprehensive care, including regular medical check-ups, adherence to medication, dietary management, and monitoring of other related conditions like hypertension and cholesterol levels.

**Hypertension**

Hypertension, or high blood pressure, is a prevalent condition among older adults and a significant risk factor for cardiovascular diseases. Age-related changes in blood vessels, such as reduced elasticity and plaque buildup, contribute to elevated blood pressure.

- **Causes and Risk Factors**: Factors contributing to hypertension include genetics, high sodium intake, lack of physical activity, obesity, and stress. Over time, hypertension can damage blood vessels and organs, particularly the heart, kidneys, and brain, leading to complications like heart attacks, stroke, and kidney disease.

- **Symptoms and Diagnosis**: Hypertension is often called a "silent killer" because it rarely causes noticeable symptoms until it has reached an advanced stage or caused significant damage. Regular blood pressure monitoring is essential for elderly individuals to detect hypertension early. Blood pressure readings consistently above 130/80 mm Hg are generally considered hypertensive, although these thresholds may vary slightly based on individual health conditions.

- **Management and Treatment**: Hypertension management for the elderly includes lifestyle changes like reducing salt intake, losing weight, avoiding smoking, managing stress, and engaging in regular exercise. Medications such as ACE inhibitors, beta-blockers, and calcium channel blockers may be prescribed to maintain optimal blood pressure levels. Regular monitoring and adherence to treatment are crucial to prevent complications, and individualized treatment plans are often required to balance multiple medications and avoid side effects.

**Cardiovascular Diseases**

Cardiovascular diseases (CVD) encompass a range of conditions affecting the heart and blood vessels, including coronary artery disease, heart failure, and arrhythmias. The risk of developing CVD increases with age due to factors such as atherosclerosis (plaque buildup in arteries), hypertension, diabetes, and lifestyle factors.

- **Coronary Artery Disease (CAD)**: CAD occurs when plaque buildup restricts blood flow to the heart, leading to chest pain (angina) and increasing the risk of heart attacks. Elderly individuals with CAD often require medications like statins and beta-blockers, along with lifestyle changes to reduce plaque formation and improve heart health.

- **Heart Failure**: This condition arises when the heart cannot pump blood effectively, leading to symptoms like shortness of breath, fatigue, and fluid retention. In older adults, heart failure is often managed through medications, dietary adjustments, and in some cases, surgical interventions.

- **Arrhythmias**: Irregular heartbeats are common among older adults and can increase the risk of stroke or sudden cardiac arrest. Conditions like atrial fibrillation may require medications to control heart rhythm and anticoagulants to prevent blood clots.

Preventing cardiovascular disease in the elderly involves managing risk factors such as hypertension, high cholesterol, diabetes, and maintaining an active lifestyle. Regular check-ups and cardiovascular screenings are essential in detecting early signs of disease.

**Respiratory Conditions**

Aging affects lung function, making respiratory diseases such as chronic obstructive pulmonary disease (COPD) and asthma common among older adults.

- **Chronic Obstructive Pulmonary Disease (COPD)**: COPD includes conditions like chronic bronchitis and emphysema, characterized by difficulty in breathing, chronic cough, and mucus production. Smoking is a leading cause of COPD, and symptoms may worsen over time, severely impacting quality of life. Treatment involves smoking cessation, bronchodilator medications, pulmonary rehabilitation, and oxygen therapy in severe cases.

- **Pneumonia**: Elderly individuals are at a higher risk for pneumonia, which can lead to severe complications and even be life-threatening. The immune system weakens with age, making it harder for the body to fight infections.

Vaccination, good hygiene, and prompt treatment of respiratory symptoms are essential preventive measures.

**Osteoporosis and Falls**

Osteoporosis, a condition characterized by low bone density and fragile bones, is particularly common among elderly women. It increases the risk of fractures, especially in the hip, spine, and wrist.

- **Causes and Risk Factors**: Osteoporosis is often caused by hormonal changes, particularly in post-menopausal women, as well as inadequate calcium and vitamin D intake. Physical inactivity, smoking, and excessive alcohol consumption are also contributing factors.

- **Management and Prevention**: Bone density scans (DEXA scans) are commonly used to diagnose osteoporosis in elderly individuals. Preventing osteoporosis involves a combination of calcium and vitamin D supplementation, weight-bearing exercises, and medications like bisphosphonates. Preventing falls is equally important, as falls can lead to severe fractures and complications. Home modifications, balance training, and vision correction can help reduce the risk of falls.

**Cognitive Decline and Neurological Disorders**

Cognitive decline is another significant concern among elderly populations. Age-related cognitive changes can range from mild forgetfulness to severe conditions such as dementia and Alzheimer's disease.

- **Dementia and Alzheimer's Disease**: Dementia is an umbrella term for a range of cognitive disorders characterized by memory loss, confusion, and impaired thinking. Alzheimer's disease is the most common form of dementia, involving the gradual loss of brain function. While no cure exists, medications and cognitive therapies can help manage symptoms and slow disease progression.

- **Parkinson's Disease**: This neurological disorder affects movement and can lead to tremors, stiffness, and difficulty with balance and coordination. Treatment often includes medications to manage symptoms and physical therapy to maintain mobility.

Cognitive health can be preserved through mental stimulation, regular exercise, a healthy diet, and social engagement. Early detection and intervention are crucial for managing neurological disorders.

### Sensory Impairments

Sensory impairments, such as vision and hearing loss, are common among older adults and can significantly impact their independence and quality of life.

- **Vision Loss**: Conditions like cataracts, glaucoma, and macular degeneration are common in old age. Regular eye exams, corrective lenses, and surgeries (such as cataract removal) can help manage these issues and improve quality of life.

- **Hearing Loss**: Age-related hearing loss, or presbycusis, affects many elderly individuals, making it difficult to communicate and increasing social isolation. Hearing aids and assistive listening devices can greatly improve hearing and social interaction.

**Digestive Health and Nutritional Concerns**

Digestive issues, such as constipation, acid reflux, and nutrient malabsorption, are also common in older adults. Reduced muscle tone, slower digestion, and changes in gut flora can lead to discomfort and nutritional deficiencies.

- **Managing Digestive Health**: A fiber-rich diet, adequate hydration, and regular physical activity can help maintain digestive health. Nutritional support, including supplements, may be necessary for elderly individuals who have difficulty absorbing certain nutrients, such as vitamin B12, calcium, and iron.
- **Malnutrition and Weight Loss**: Some elderly individuals struggle with unintentional weight loss due to decreased appetite, dental issues, or other health conditions. Monitoring nutrition and ensuring a balanced diet is essential for maintaining physical health and energy levels.

Aging brings with it a range of physical health challenges that require diligent management and individualized care. While certain health concerns, like arthritis, diabetes, and hypertension, are more common among the elderly, proper lifestyle adjustments, early detection, and adherence to treatment plans can help manage these conditions and improve quality of life. A comprehensive approach that includes regular medical check-ups, a balanced diet, physical activity, and preventive care is essential for promoting health and longevity in elderly individuals.

---

**Example 1**: Sundaram, a 74-year-old farmer, spent most of his life working in the fields. Now, he struggles with arthritis, making it challenging for him to do even simple chores. Though initially reluctant, Sundaram's son convinced him to visit a local health centre, where he was diagnosed with arthritis and hypertension. The doctor recommended gentle yoga exercises and a modified diet to manage his symptoms. With his son's encouragement, Sundaram began daily yoga classes and adjusted his diet to include more vegetables, millets, and fiber-rich foods. Over time, his pain became more manageable, and he found himself more active and mobile, enjoying time with his grandchildren in the mornings.

**Example 2**: Vijayan, a 75-year-old from rural Andhra Pradesh, recently developed severe knee pain due to arthritis, which limits his ability to move around his village as freely as he once did. His daughter, who lives in Bengaluru, arranges for a doctor's visit and convinces him to try physiotherapy exercises and pain management treatments. Though hesitant at first, Vijayan begins noticing improvement after following a daily exercise regimen and taking prescribed medication. He even starts using a simple walking stick, allowing him to visit his friends at the local tea shop every evening, gradually regaining his independence.

# Mental Health and Aging

Mental health is a crucial, though often overlooked, aspect of overall well-being among elderly individuals. Aging can bring unique challenges to mental health, influenced by physical health concerns, social isolation, loss of loved ones, and transitions in living situations. Common mental health issues among the elderly include dementia, depression, and anxiety, each impacting not only the individual's quality of life but also their physical health and ability to engage with the world around them. Understanding these mental health challenges and adopting strategies to address them can significantly improve the well-being of elderly individuals.

**Dementia and Cognitive Decline**

Dementia is a progressive decline in cognitive function, impacting memory, problem-solving, language, and other mental abilities. It is an umbrella term that includes various types, with Alzheimer's disease being the most common form. Dementia can have profound effects on an individual's daily life, independence, and ability to interact with others.

- **Types of Dementia**: While Alzheimer's disease is the most prevalent, other types of dementia include vascular dementia, dementia with Lewy bodies, and frontotemporal dementia. Each type has unique characteristics, though symptoms may overlap. Vascular dementia, for instance, is linked to reduced blood flow to the brain, often due to strokes, while Lewy body dementia is associated with abnormal protein deposits in the brain, affecting movement and cognition.

- **Causes and Risk Factors**: While age is the most significant risk factor for dementia, genetics, lifestyle, and environmental factors also play roles. Chronic health conditions like hypertension, diabetes, and obesity can increase the risk of dementia, as can lifestyle choices such as smoking, lack of physical activity, and poor diet. Protective factors, such as staying mentally active, maintaining social connections, and engaging in regular physical activity, can help reduce the risk.

- **Symptoms and Diagnosis**: Early symptoms of dementia include memory loss, difficulty with language, disorientation, and challenges in planning or organizing. Over time, individuals may experience significant personality changes, loss of motor skills, and reduced ability to care for themselves. Diagnosing dementia typically involves cognitive tests, neurological exams, and, in some cases, brain imaging.

- **Treatment and Management**: While no cure currently exists for most types of dementia, treatments focus on managing symptoms and slowing disease progression. Medications, such as cholinesterase inhibitors, can help improve cognitive symptoms in early to moderate stages. Non-pharmacological approaches, including cognitive therapy, structured routines, and social engagement, can support mental well-being. Caregivers and family members play a crucial role in providing daily support and ensuring a safe environment for those with dementia.

**Depression in Older Adults**

Depression is a common but often unrecognized mental health issue among the elderly. Unlike situational sadness, depression is a persistent mood disorder that can affect thoughts, feelings, and daily activities. Elderly individuals may be more susceptible to depression due to life transitions, loss of independence, chronic illness, and social isolation.

- **Causes and Risk Factors**: Depression in older adults can be triggered by a range of factors, including chronic physical health conditions, medications with depressive side effects, grief, and isolation. Loss of social roles or purpose after retirement, financial stress, and physical pain can also contribute to feelings of hopelessness and low self-worth.

- **Symptoms and Diagnosis**: Depression in elderly individuals may manifest differently than in younger populations. Common symptoms include persistent sadness, lack of interest in previously enjoyed activities, fatigue, sleep disturbances, weight changes, and feelings of worthlessness. In some cases, depression may present as physical complaints, such as unexplained aches and pains. Diagnosing depression in the elderly can be challenging, as symptoms may overlap with other health issues. Tools like the Geriatric Depression Scale (GDS) can help healthcare providers assess depression in older adults.

- **Treatment and Management**: Treating depression in older adults often involves a combination of medications, such as selective serotonin reuptake inhibitors (SSRIs), and psychotherapy, including cognitive-behavioural therapy (CBT). Regular physical activity, engaging in hobbies, and maintaining social connections can help improve mood and reduce depressive symptoms. Support from family members, counselling, and community involvement also play essential roles in recovery.

**Anxiety Disorders in the Elderly**

Anxiety is another prevalent mental health concern among older adults, affecting their ability to cope with daily life. Anxiety disorders can range from generalized anxiety disorder (GAD) to phobias and panic disorders. Aging-related changes and fears, such as worries about health, finances, and independence, can increase anxiety levels in elderly individuals.

- **Types and Symptoms**: Common forms of anxiety in older adults include generalized anxiety disorder, characterized by excessive worry; panic disorder, with sudden episodes of intense fear; and phobias, where individuals may develop specific fears (such as of falling). Symptoms of anxiety disorders in elderly individuals include restlessness, excessive worrying, irritability, muscle tension, and difficulty concentrating.

- **Causes and Risk Factors**: Anxiety in the elderly may stem from various sources, including health concerns, loss of loved ones, physical limitations, and changes in living environments. Those with a history of anxiety earlier in life may experience a recurrence or worsening of symptoms as they age. Chronic health conditions, social isolation, and certain medications can also exacerbate anxiety.

- **Treatment and Management**: Anxiety disorders are often managed through a combination of psychotherapy and, in some cases, medication. Cognitive-behavioural therapy is highly effective in helping individuals identify and manage anxious thoughts. Mindfulness practices, relaxation techniques, and regular exercise can reduce anxiety symptoms. Family support and reassurance can also help elderly individuals feel more secure and less anxious about uncertainties.

## Social Isolation and Loneliness

Social isolation and loneliness are significant risk factors for mental health issues among the elderly. The loss of friends and family members, retirement, reduced mobility, and the transition to assisted living or long-term care facilities can all contribute to feelings of loneliness. Studies show that social isolation not only increases the risk of depression and anxiety but is also linked to cognitive decline, dementia, and even mortality.

- **Impact of Social Isolation**: Loneliness and social isolation can lead to chronic stress, which negatively affects the body and mind. Prolonged isolation can weaken the immune system, increase blood pressure, and contribute to physical and mental health decline. Elderly individuals who lack social interactions may be at higher risk of developing depression, cognitive decline, and poor physical health.

- **Preventing Social Isolation**: Creating social opportunities for elderly individuals, such as through community centres, senior groups, and family involvement, can help combat isolation. Technology can also play a role, allowing elderly individuals to stay connected with family and friends through video calls and social media. Intergenerational programs that connect elderly individuals with younger people, including children and teenagers, can foster meaningful relationships and reduce loneliness.

**The Role of Physical Health in Mental Well-being**

Physical health and mental well-being are closely linked. Chronic illnesses, pain, and reduced mobility can contribute to mental health challenges, including depression and anxiety. Elderly individuals facing multiple physical health issues may feel a loss of control, independence, and self-worth, all of which can negatively impact mental health.

- **Physical Activity and Mental Health**: Regular physical activity has been shown to improve mood, reduce anxiety, and help with symptoms of depression. Exercise increases endorphins, reduces stress, and helps elderly individuals feel more energetic and confident. For those with limited mobility, gentle exercises like stretching, yoga, and seated exercises can provide both physical and mental health benefits.

- **Managing Chronic Pain**: Chronic pain can be a significant source of stress and mental distress for elderly individuals. Effective pain management, including medication, physical therapy, and alternative therapies such as acupuncture and mindfulness, can help alleviate the mental burden of chronic pain.

## Sleep Disorders and Their Impact on Mental Health

Sleep disorders, including insomnia and sleep apnea, are common among elderly individuals and can have a profound impact on mental health. Poor sleep quality can lead to irritability, cognitive decline, depression, and anxiety, making it essential to address sleep issues.

- **Causes of Sleep Disorders**: Changes in circadian rhythms, medications, physical discomfort, and underlying health conditions all contribute to sleep difficulties in older adults. Environmental factors, such as noise, lighting, and temperature, can also disrupt sleep.

- **Improving Sleep Quality**: Good sleep hygiene practices, such as maintaining a consistent sleep schedule, reducing caffeine intake, and creating a relaxing bedtime routine, can help improve sleep quality. Treating underlying conditions, such as sleep apnea with CPAP therapy, is also crucial for achieving restful sleep.

**Promoting Mental Health and Well-being in Elderly Populations**

Addressing the mental health needs of elderly individuals requires a multi-faceted approach. Family members, healthcare providers, and communities play essential roles in supporting mental well-being and improving quality of life. Some key strategies include:

- **Early Detection and Intervention**: Regular mental health screenings for older adults can help identify symptoms of depression, anxiety, and dementia early on, allowing for timely intervention and treatment. Tools like the Geriatric Depression Scale and the Mini-Mental State Examination are useful for assessing mental health in the elderly.

- **Community Programs and Support Groups**: Community centres, senior programs, and support groups provide elderly individuals with opportunities to connect with others, reducing loneliness and offering a sense of belonging. Social engagement is crucial for mental well-being and can help elderly individuals maintain cognitive and emotional health.

- **Promoting Independence and Autonomy**: Encouraging elderly individuals to make decisions about their own lives, whether related to daily activities, medical care, or hobbies, can improve their sense of control and reduce stress. Independence is a critical factor in self-esteem and mental health among older adults.

- **Education for Caregivers**: Family members and caregivers benefit from education on how to support elderly individuals with mental health challenges. Training on recognizing symptoms, effective communication, and stress management can improve care quality and reduce caregiver burnout.

Mental health is a vital component of healthy aging, and addressing mental health concerns in the elderly is essential for maintaining a high quality of life. By understanding the unique mental health challenges older adults face, such as dementia, depression, and anxiety, caregivers and family members can provide better support, empathy, and resources to help them thrive. Comprehensive care, including early detection, personalized treatment, social support, and family involvement, can positively impact the mental health and overall well-being of elderly individuals, helping them to lead fulfilling lives as they age.

---

**Example 1**: Kamala, a 76-year-old widow from Coimbatore, started experiencing memory lapses and forgetfulness. As the weeks went by, her children began noticing her increasing confusion and irritability. After a few incidents, such as forgetting to turn off the stove and misplacing important documents, her family decided to seek medical help. Kamala was diagnosed with early-stage dementia. Her family now actively involves her in memory-stimulating activities and ensures she has a daily routine to reduce confusion. With time, her family has become more understanding, adjusting their communication style to make her feel heard and valued, ensuring that Kamala still feels connected and supported.

**Example 2**: Saraswati, an 81-year-old, recently lost her husband of 60 years. Living with her son's family in Chennai, she finds herself feeling isolated, despite being surrounded by loved ones. She spends hours alone, reminiscing about the life she once shared with her husband. Recognizing her need for social interaction, her granddaughter encourages her to join a neighbourhood senior's club, where she meets other elderly women who have gone through similar losses. Over time, Saraswati begins to feel a sense of community and support, finding comfort and mental peace in her shared experiences with others

# Nutritional Needs of the Elderly

Nutrition is a cornerstone of health, particularly for elderly individuals who face unique physiological and lifestyle changes. As people age, they may experience a decrease in appetite, changes in taste and smell, or difficulties in preparing meals, all of which can impact their nutritional intake. Meeting the dietary needs of elderly individuals is essential for maintaining energy, supporting immune function, and reducing the risk of chronic diseases and other health issues. Traditional diets, cultural practices, and awareness of nutritional gaps all play roles in addressing the specific dietary needs of elderly individuals.

**Understanding the Nutritional Requirements of the Elderly**

Aging leads to changes in body composition, metabolism, and digestion, all of which can affect nutritional needs. As muscle mass decreases and metabolic rates slow down, elderly individuals may require fewer calories but need more nutrient-dense foods to meet their dietary needs. Key nutritional considerations include protein, vitamins and minerals, fiber, and adequate hydration, each serving specific functions for physical and mental health.

- **Protein**: Protein is essential for maintaining muscle mass and repairing tissues, which is critical in preventing muscle wasting and weakness in the elderly. The reduction in muscle mass due to aging, known as sarcopenia, increases the risk of falls and fractures. Lean protein sources like fish,

poultry, legumes, and dairy are beneficial, while plant-based proteins are useful for those with dietary restrictions or low appetites.
- **Vitamins and Minerals**: Certain micronutrients are vital for elderly individuals, including vitamin D, calcium, B vitamins, and antioxidants like vitamins C and E. Vitamin D and calcium are crucial for bone health, while B vitamins, particularly B6 and B12, support cognitive function, nerve health, and red blood cell formation. Antioxidants protect against cellular damage from oxidative stress, which can contribute to age-related diseases.

- **Fiber**: Fiber supports digestive health, preventing constipation and reducing the risk of diverticular disease, which becomes more common with age. Whole grains, fruits, and vegetables are excellent sources of fiber, and a high-fiber diet is also beneficial for managing cholesterol levels and blood sugar, which is crucial for elderly individuals with cardiovascular disease or diabetes.
- **Hydration**: Elderly individuals are at a higher risk of dehydration due to decreased thirst sensitivity, potential kidney function changes, and medications that may cause fluid loss. Proper hydration supports kidney function, cognitive performance, and joint health. Water, herbal teas, and soups are excellent hydration sources, while sugary drinks and caffeine are best limited.

## Traditional South Indian Diets and Their Benefits for the Elderly

The South Indian diet, rich in plant-based foods, spices, and moderate protein sources, provides many nutrients necessary for healthy aging. Traditional diets typically emphasize a balance of carbohydrates, protein, and healthy fats with an abundance of vegetables, legumes, and grains, often accompanied by fermented foods, which are beneficial for gut health.

- **Staple Foods and Their Nutrients**: South Indian diets usually include rice, millet, lentils, and vegetables, which are rich in fiber, vitamins, and minerals. Lentils, such as dal, provide plant-based protein and iron, while rice is a good carbohydrate source. Incorporating millet can offer more fiber, protein, and essential minerals than traditional white rice, which is beneficial for blood sugar management.
- **Spices with Health Benefits**: Spices like turmeric, cumin, and ginger are commonly used in South Indian cuisine and possess anti-inflammatory and antioxidant properties. Turmeric, in particular, is high in curcumin, a compound with numerous health benefits, including joint health, reduced inflammation, and improved brain health.
- **Fermented Foods**: Fermented foods like idli, dosa, and buttermilk are staples of the diet. Fermentation promotes beneficial gut bacteria, supporting digestive health and immunity. Fermented foods can also improve nutrient absorption, which is beneficial for elderly individuals who may face nutrient malabsorption.

**Nutritional Gaps in Elderly Diets**

Despite the benefits of a traditional diet, elderly individuals may face nutritional gaps due to a decrease in appetite, dietary restrictions, or physical limitations in meal preparation. Common deficiencies include vitamin D, B vitamins, calcium, iron, and protein.

- **Vitamin D and Calcium Deficiency**: Vitamin D deficiency is common due to limited sun exposure and dietary intake. In combination with insufficient calcium, this can increase the risk of osteoporosis and bone fractures. Dairy products, fortified foods, and supplements can help address these deficiencies. Ensuring 15-30 minutes of sun exposure daily is also beneficial, although this may not be possible for all elderly individuals.
- **Vitamin B12 Deficiency**: As the body ages, it produces less stomach acid, which is necessary for absorbing vitamin B12. This deficiency can lead to anaemia and neurological issues, affecting balance and memory. Foods rich in B12, like dairy, eggs, fish, and fortified cereals, are recommended. Elderly individuals with significant absorption issues may benefit from B12 injections or high-dose oral supplements.
- **Protein Deficiency**: Elderly individuals often consume less protein than required due to chewing difficulties, reduced appetite, or limited access to protein-rich foods. Protein deficiency can contribute to muscle wasting, decreased immune function, and slower recovery from illness or injury. Small, frequent servings of soft protein-rich foods, such as yogurt, scrambled eggs, or lentil soups, can help meet protein needs.
- **Iron and Anaemia**: Iron deficiency can lead to anaemia, causing fatigue, weakness, and cognitive difficulties. Consuming iron-rich foods such as lentils, spinach, and nuts, along with vitamin C sources to improve absorption, can help prevent anaemia.

**Challenges in Meeting Nutritional Needs**

Various challenges can affect the nutritional intake of elderly individuals, ranging from medical and physical limitations to socio-economic factors.

- **Loss of Appetite and Sensory Decline**: Aging can dull the senses of taste and smell, making food less appealing. Medications and illnesses can also contribute to appetite loss. Small, frequent meals and flavour-enhancing spices can make meals more palatable.
- **Chewing and Swallowing Difficulties**: Dental issues, dry mouth, and swallowing difficulties are common among the elderly, impacting food intake. Soft foods, pureed vegetables, and smoothies provide nutrients without causing discomfort.
- **Economic and Accessibility Issues**: Elderly individuals on a limited income may struggle to afford nutritious foods, particularly if they have restricted mobility or limited access to fresh produce. Local community programs, grocery delivery services, and support from family members can help address these challenges.
- **Medication and Nutrient Interactions**: Many medications have side effects that impact nutrient absorption, appetite, or hydration. Healthcare providers can offer guidance on managing these interactions, potentially adjusting doses or suggesting supplements to counteract deficiencies.

**Strategies for Addressing Nutritional Gaps**

Identifying and addressing nutritional gaps is essential for improving the health and quality of life of elderly individuals. Practical strategies can make healthy eating more accessible and enjoyable, even in the face of common aging challenges.

- **Meal Planning and Preparation**: Preparing meals in advance or freezing single portions can make nutritious meals readily available. Community programs or family members can assist with meal preparation, reducing the burden on elderly individuals.
- **Incorporating Nutrient-Dense Foods**: Small adjustments to traditional diets can provide nutrient-dense meals. Adding nuts, seeds, and leafy greens to curries, soups, or rice dishes boosts nutrient content without requiring significant changes to flavour or food preparation.
- **Using Nutritional Supplements**: When dietary changes alone cannot address deficiencies, supplements can provide essential nutrients. Common supplements for the elderly include vitamin D, calcium, and B vitamins, but these should be used under the supervision of a healthcare provider.
- **Promoting Hydration**: Encouraging fluid intake throughout the day is essential. Soups, herbal teas, and fruit-based drinks can provide hydration and nutrients. In hot climates, drinking water with added electrolytes can help prevent dehydration.

## The Role of Family and Community in Supporting Elderly Nutrition

Family members and caregivers play a crucial role in supporting elderly individuals' nutritional needs, helping ensure they consume balanced and nutritious meals regularly. In urban families, where multi-generational living is common, family members can easily assist elderly individuals with food shopping, meal preparation, and even encouraging meal times.

- **Cultural Food Practices**: Embracing traditional foods that are culturally familiar can enhance the eating experience for elderly individuals, making meals more enjoyable. For example, elderly individuals who prefer traditional meals may respond positively to familiar dishes that meet their nutritional needs, such as idli with vegetable-rich sambar, or dosa with lentil chutney.
- **Community Support Programs**: Many urban areas now offer community programs that provide healthy meals or nutrition education for elderly individuals. Community centres, senior groups, and local NGOs can offer meal delivery services or workshops on cooking and nutrition tailored to older adults. Such programs can also foster social engagement, encouraging elderly individuals to participate in communal meals and social events.

Meeting the nutritional needs of elderly individuals requires a holistic approach that considers physical, cultural, and social factors. Traditional diets offer a solid foundation for balanced nutrition, but nutritional gaps often arise due to physiological changes, lifestyle adjustments, and limited access to nutrient-dense foods. By addressing these gaps through dietary adjustments, supplements, family support, and community programs, elderly individuals can maintain their health, strength, and independence. Ultimately, good nutrition plays a fundamental role in enhancing the quality of life and well-being of elderly individuals as they navigate the challenges of aging.

> **Example 1**: Narayana, an 80-year-old from Madurai, had a diet rich in white rice and coconut-based curries all his life. Recently, he started experiencing digestive issues, fatigue, and weight loss. Upon consulting with a nutritionist, he learned that his aging body required more balanced nutrition to meet his changing dietary needs. The nutritionist suggested switching some meals to incorporate fiber-rich foods like ragi (millet) and vegetables, along with protein-rich foods such as dals and yogurt. Narayana's daughter-in-law began preparing a daily bowl of vegetable and dal stew, which helped improve his digestion. Small changes, like substituting white rice with millets in some meals, made a significant difference, and he began feeling more energetic and healthier.
>
> **Example 2**: Ranganayaki, an 82-year-old from Coimbatore, grew up on a diet rich in ghee, sweets, and rice. After a recent health check-up, her doctor advised a change to lighter, more nutrient-rich foods to help with her digestion and prevent fatigue. Her daughter-in-law steps in to make subtle changes, adding dishes like steamed vegetables, lentil-based curries, and yogurt to her meals while gradually reducing the portion of rice. She even makes idlis with millet flour for breakfast instead of rice, which Ranganayaki finds surprisingly enjoyable. Over time, she feels more energetic and looks forward to her meals, appreciating how her diet still retains the Flavours she loves.

# Physical Fitness and Mobility for the Elderly

Maintaining physical activity and mobility in old age is crucial to fostering a healthy, independent, and fulfilling life. Aging is a natural process that inevitably brings about physical changes, often diminishing strength, balance, and flexibility. However, consistent physical activity and mobility can significantly counteract many of these effects, helping seniors preserve their independence and quality of life. For elderly individuals, physical fitness isn't merely about aesthetics or athleticism but is essential for functional health, psychological well-being, and social engagement.

**The Importance of Physical Fitness in Old Age**

Physical fitness is the foundation of vitality, impacting not only the body but also the mind. As we age, our metabolism slows down, and muscle mass and bone density gradually decrease. For the elderly, maintaining physical fitness is fundamental to combating these declines and ensuring that the body continues to perform essential functions with minimal strain or discomfort. Physical fitness in old age isn't about rigorous workouts but about sustaining mobility, flexibility, and strength through activities that are safe, enjoyable, and beneficial for health.

## a) Strength and Muscle Health

Loss of muscle mass, or sarcopenia, is a common issue among the elderly, contributing to frailty and an increased risk of falls. Gentle strength-training exercises can help combat this decline, improving balance and overall stability. For instance, simple exercises like bodyweight squats, arm raises, and resistance band routines can promote muscle maintenance and strength without stressing the joints. Elderly individuals who engage in such strength-based activities often experience enhanced energy, endurance, and confidence in handling daily tasks.

## b) Bone Density and Joint Health

Osteoporosis and arthritis are prevalent among seniors, with weakened bones and joint degeneration leading to stiffness and discomfort. Exercises like walking, tai chi, or light dancing can strengthen bones and maintain joint flexibility. Research indicates that weight-bearing exercises help improve bone density, reducing the risk of fractures. Additionally, joint-friendly activities like swimming provide a full-body workout without straining the joints, making them ideal for elderly individuals.

## c) Balance and Fall Prevention

Balance deteriorates with age, increasing the likelihood of falls, which can lead to fractures and serious health complications. Incorporating exercises that focus on balance, such as yoga, tai chi, or even basic balance exercises (like standing on one leg), can enhance stability and coordination. Improved balance not only reduces the risk of falls but also promotes confidence in movement, encouraging seniors to remain active.

**Mobility: A Pillar of Independence**

Mobility is closely tied to quality of life and independence. It encompasses the body's ability to move freely and perform everyday activities, such as walking, climbing stairs, and getting in and out of a chair. When mobility is compromised, so is an individual's ability to live independently and confidently. Prioritizing mobility through appropriate exercises and lifestyle adjustments can significantly prolong the period of independence in old age.

**a) Flexibility and Range of Motion**

Regular stretching is essential for preserving flexibility and a full range of motion, which becomes increasingly important with age. Stretching exercises keep muscles and joints supple, reducing stiffness and pain. Simple stretches for the legs, back, and arms can make a world of difference, allowing seniors to move comfortably and accomplish tasks like bending to tie shoelaces or reaching overhead shelves without discomfort.

**b) Improving Cardiovascular Health**

Mobility is often hindered by poor cardiovascular health, leading to fatigue and shortness of breath during movement. Cardiovascular exercises, tailored to an individual's fitness level, improve heart and lung function. Walking, cycling, or low-impact aerobic exercises increase circulation, stamina, and endurance, enhancing both physical and mental well-being. These activities are also linked to a reduction in blood pressure and cholesterol levels, contributing to overall heart health.

### c) Maintaining Balance and Coordination

As mobility declines, so do balance and coordination, which are crucial for walking steadily and navigating uneven surfaces. Balance exercises help seniors remain agile, reducing the risk of falls and injuries. Functional mobility exercises, such as stepping over obstacles or practicing stair climbing, can improve the brain's communication with muscles, allowing for smoother and safer movements.

### The Psychological and Social Benefits of Physical Activity

Physical fitness extends beyond physical health; it impacts the psychological and social well-being of elderly individuals. Regular activity enhances mood, reduces anxiety and depression, and provides a sense of achievement and purpose. For the elderly, physical activity often brings structure to the day, fosters social connections, and improves cognitive functions.

### a) Boosting Mental Health and Cognitive Function

Exercise releases endorphins, which act as natural mood enhancers. Regular physical activity has been shown to reduce symptoms of depression, improve sleep quality, and increase feelings of relaxation. Engaging in fitness activities also improves cognitive health by promoting blood flow to the brain, aiding memory and mental clarity. Activities that involve coordination or strategic thinking, such as yoga or dance, can also stimulate the brain, reducing the risk of cognitive decline.

## b) Encouraging Social Engagement

For many seniors, group activities like yoga classes, walking groups, or swimming sessions at community centres provide a social outlet. These gatherings create opportunities to build friendships, discuss shared experiences, and enjoy mutual encouragement. Group physical activities enhance social bonds and provide a support system that is especially important for seniors who might feel isolated.

## c) Fostering a Sense of Purpose

Setting and achieving fitness goals can instil a sense of accomplishment and purpose. Elderly individuals who work towards small milestones, such as walking an extra block or lifting a slightly heavier weight, experience a boost in self-esteem. Regular fitness activities encourage seniors to set personal goals, empowering them to take charge of their health and wellness, reinforcing a positive self-image.

## Practical Approaches to Physical Fitness for the Elderly

Promoting physical fitness and mobility among the elderly involves a balance of safe, enjoyable activities that cater to their specific health needs. The following are practical approaches to implementing fitness routines that foster strength, flexibility, and endurance:

### a) Walking: The Simple, Powerful Exercise

Walking is one of the easiest and most accessible forms of exercise. Seniors can adjust their pace and duration according to their fitness level, and it doesn't require any special equipment. Regular walking enhances cardiovascular fitness, boosts mood, and strengthens leg muscles, promoting stability and balance. Walking with friends, family, or a pet can also make the experience enjoyable and socially fulfilling.

### b) Gentle Yoga and Tai Chi

Yoga and tai chi are particularly beneficial for seniors, focusing on balance, flexibility, and mental relaxation. These practices are slow-paced, mindful, and can be easily adapted to accommodate physical limitations. Yoga poses and tai chi movements improve core strength, body awareness, and breathing, which are crucial for maintaining coordination and mobility. Many seniors find these practices calming and uplifting, enhancing both physical and mental resilience.

### c) Resistance and Strength Training

Simple strength-training exercises, using light weights or resistance bands, help preserve muscle mass and bone density. For instance, chair exercises, arm curls, or seated leg raises strengthen core and limb muscles without requiring extensive movement. Regular strength training fosters independence, enabling seniors to handle daily activities like carrying groceries or standing up from a seated position.

### d) Stretching and Flexibility Exercises

Incorporating stretching exercises into a daily routine keeps the muscles and joints limber, reducing stiffness and pain. Stretches targeting the lower back, hamstrings, and shoulders are particularly beneficial for maintaining mobility. Even a brief morning or evening stretching session can improve range of motion, prevent injuries, and reduce discomfort in everyday tasks.

### e) Aqua Aerobics and Swimming

Water-based exercises are low-impact and gentle on the joints, making them ideal for seniors with arthritis or joint pain. Swimming and aqua aerobics offer a full-body workout, improving cardiovascular health, flexibility, and strength. The buoyancy of water supports body weight, reducing strain and minimizing the risk of injury. Many community pools offer senior-focused aqua classes, which provide a fun, engaging, and safe environment.

### Safety Tips for Elderly Physical Activity

For seniors, safety is paramount when engaging in physical activities. Medical consultation, proper warm-up, gradual progression, and awareness of one's limits are key to a safe and effective fitness regimen.

- **Consult a Healthcare Professional**: Before starting any new exercise routine, elderly individuals should consult their doctor to ensure the exercises align with their health needs.
- **Warm-Up and Cool-Down**: Proper warm-up and cool-down help prepare the muscles for movement and prevent injuries.
- **Stay Hydrated**: Seniors should remember to stay hydrated, especially during physical activities, to avoid fatigue or dizziness.
- **Use Proper Equipment**: Supportive footwear, resistance bands, or light weights enhance safety and effectiveness.
- **Listen to the Body**: If an activity causes pain or discomfort, it's important to stop and reassess. Gentle exercises that are pain-free are most effective.

Physical fitness and mobility are the foundations of healthy aging, allowing seniors to retain independence, enhance well-being, and experience life to the fullest. The benefits of physical activity are vast, extending beyond the physical to enrich mental health, social engagement, and self-worth. While the journey may vary for each individual, the importance of staying active, regardless of age, cannot be overstated. Through simple, consistent movement and community support, seniors can look forward to aging gracefully, with strength, resilience, and joy.

---

**Example 1**: Venkatesan, a 76-year-old from Madurai, had always led an active life as a farmer, but after moving to the city to live with his son's family, he became mostly sedentary. Over time, he found it increasingly difficult to walk without assistance, experiencing knee pain and stiffness in his joints. Venkatesan's daughter-in-law noticed his reduced mobility and suggested he start with short, daily walks around their apartment complex. At first, Venkatesan struggled to complete even a single lap, but with encouragement from his family, he gradually began extending his walks. His grandchildren joined him, making it an enjoyable part of his day. Over a few months, Venkatesan found his knee pain reduced, and his stamina improved. His confidence soared as he began taking longer walks and even joining a group of senior friends for morning strolls at the nearby park. Venkatesan rediscovered his independence, feeling both physically stronger and mentally refreshed.

**Example 2**: Lakshmi, an 82-year-old widow from Bengaluru, struggled with daily activities like carrying groceries, lifting utensils, and even standing up from her chair due to muscle weakness. Her son suggested she try strength training exercises with a physiotherapist, who introduced her to gentle exercises using resistance bands and small weights. Lakshmi started with simple arm and leg lifts, initially finding the exercises challenging. However, she was determined to regain her self-sufficiency. After weeks of practice, she began noticing improvements in her muscle strength and balance, enabling her to perform daily tasks more comfortably. Lakshmi's confidence increased, and she could once again move around her home and community independently, without constantly relying on others for help. Her newfound strength transformed her daily life, giving her a sense of accomplishment and pride in her abilities.

# Access to Healthcare and Geriatric Services

Access to healthcare and geriatric services is essential for elderly individuals, particularly in urban areas where lifestyle changes and the shift from joint to nuclear families have increased the elderly population's need for medical care and support. However, elderly individuals face numerous challenges when accessing healthcare services, from logistical barriers to the limited availability of specialized geriatric care.

With advancements in medical science and increased awareness of age-related health needs, cities across South India, such as Chennai, Bengaluru, and Hyderabad, have begun implementing specialized services. Yet, significant challenges remain, limiting many seniors' ability to access and benefit from healthcare resources effectively.

**Common Healthcare Needs of the Elderly**

As people age, their healthcare needs become more complex, often requiring a combination of routine and specialized medical attention. Common health issues that urban elderly individuals face include:

- **Chronic Illnesses**: Conditions like diabetes, hypertension, and cardiovascular diseases are prevalent among the

elderly, often necessitating regular check-ups, medication, and lifestyle adjustments.
- **Joint and Mobility Issues**: Osteoarthritis, osteoporosis, and mobility limitations are common, requiring physiotherapy, pain management, or assistive devices like walkers and wheelchairs.
- **Mental Health Concerns**: Depression, anxiety, and cognitive decline, including dementia, are also prominent issues, especially for elderly individuals living alone or isolated from family members.
- **Vision and Hearing Loss**: Age-related changes in sight and hearing can limit the independence of elderly individuals and require specialized devices or corrective surgery.
- **Preventive Care**: Regular screenings for cancers, vaccinations (like flu shots), and bone density tests are critical for preventive healthcare in the elderly, ensuring early detection of potential issues.

The combination of these health needs requires an integrated approach to geriatric healthcare, which can be challenging for elderly individuals to access due to various systemic and social barriers.

**Challenges in Accessing Healthcare for the Urban Elderly**

Urban elderly individuals face several unique challenges in accessing healthcare, despite being in proximity to healthcare facilities. Some of the key barriers include:

## a) Financial Constraints

For many elderly individuals, financial independence is limited. Without a steady income, they rely on pensions or family support, which may not be sufficient to cover medical expenses. Though some urban elderly individuals may be covered by family health insurance plans, the costs of chronic disease management, hospital visits, specialized therapies, and medications can still impose a heavy financial burden. Furthermore, private hospitals and specialized care facilities often charge premiums that are beyond the reach of many seniors, making healthcare access unaffordable.

## b) Limited Mobility and Transport

For urban elderly individuals with mobility issues, commuting to hospitals or clinics can be a daunting task. Public transportation may not be senior-friendly, and options like taxis or rideshares can be costly and challenging for seniors with limited mobility. Additionally, elderly individuals with chronic joint pain or cardiovascular issues may struggle to sit through long waiting periods, making them hesitant to visit healthcare facilities without assistance.

## c) Inadequate Awareness and Health Literacy

Health literacy can be a barrier for elderly individuals unfamiliar with the nuances of modern healthcare systems. Many elderly people may not fully understand complex medical information, medication requirements, or follow-up care instructions. This can lead to poor medication adherence, delayed treatment, and increased risk of complications. Moreover, a lack of awareness about available services or government-supported programs often keeps elderly individuals from receiving the assistance they need.

**d) Social Isolation and Lack of Family Support**

In urban areas, the transition from joint to nuclear families has left many elderly people without close family support. Elderly individuals who live alone may find it difficult to attend medical appointments, take medications on time, or make informed healthcare decisions. Social isolation can also exacerbate mental health issues, creating a cycle of disengagement from necessary healthcare services.

**e) Insufficient Geriatric Specialists and Facilities**

Despite the growing elderly population, there remains a shortage of geriatric specialists and dedicated facilities that cater to elderly healthcare needs. The focus in many urban healthcare centres remains on acute, general medical care, rather than holistic, specialized geriatric services that can manage age-related complexities. As a result, elderly patients may end up in emergency rooms or general wards, where care may not be fully tailored to their requirements.

**Availability of Specialized Geriatric Services**

In recent years, there has been an increasing acknowledgment of the need for dedicated geriatric services in South Indian cities. Some initiatives have been made, both at the private and government levels, to address elderly healthcare needs more effectively.

### a) Geriatric Clinics and Hospitals

Several urban hospitals have established specialized geriatric departments staffed by healthcare professionals trained in elderly care. These clinics offer services tailored to the elderly, including:

- **Comprehensive Health Assessments**: Routine health check-ups designed to assess the physical, mental, and cognitive health of elderly individuals.
- **Medication Management**: Monitoring prescriptions and adjusting medications to prevent side effects and interactions that are more common in the elderly.
- **Physical Rehabilitation Services**: Physiotherapy, occupational therapy, and mobility training programs to help seniors maintain functional independence.

In cities like Chennai and Bengaluru, major hospitals, such as Apollo and Manipal, have introduced geriatric care programs, and specific geriatric clinics have emerged, although accessibility is often limited to those who can afford private care.

### b) Home Healthcare Services

Home healthcare has become an increasingly popular option for elderly individuals in urban areas. Services like Kites, Portea, Nightingales, and HealthCare at Home offer in-home medical care, including routine health assessments, physiotherapy, post-operative care, and chronic disease management. These services bring healthcare to the elderly's doorstep, which is especially beneficial for those with mobility constraints or those living alone. Home healthcare is a growing sector in India, though it can be costly and is not covered by many insurance plans.

### c) Telemedicine and Digital Health Platforms

With the advent of telemedicine, elderly individuals can now access medical consultations without leaving their homes. Platforms such as Practo, mfine, and DocsApp connect patients with doctors via video or audio calls, allowing elderly individuals to consult with specialists without facing transportation barriers. Telemedicine has been particularly effective in managing chronic diseases, where regular monitoring and medication adjustments are required. However, the elderly often need assistance navigating these digital platforms, which may not be senior-friendly.

### d) Government-Supported Programs and Clinics

In some states, government-supported programs provide subsidized healthcare services for the elderly. For instance, the National Programme for Health Care of the Elderly (NPHCE) aims to deliver primary, secondary, and tertiary healthcare to seniors, including preventive, diagnostic, and therapeutic services. Primary healthcare centres (PHCs) in urban areas provide free consultations and medicines for common age-related ailments. However, these programs are often understaffed and lack the resources needed for comprehensive geriatric care.

### e) Daycare Centres and Senior Care Facilities

In metropolitan areas, a few senior daycare centres and residential care facilities provide support for elderly individuals who need companionship, supervision, or medical care during the day. These facilities, such as Aware Senior Care and Athulya Assisted Living, offer structured programs that include exercise, recreation, and health monitoring. They provide a social environment for the elderly while meeting their healthcare needs. These centres are helpful, especially for families that cannot offer full-time care at home.

## Strategies for Improving Healthcare Access for Urban Elderly

Enhancing healthcare access for the elderly population requires a multi-faceted approach involving community involvement, healthcare providers, government support, and family awareness. The following strategies could improve healthcare accessibility for urban elderly:

### a) Developing Affordable Healthcare Plans
Insurance companies and government programs could introduce affordable healthcare plans tailored for elderly individuals. Subsidizing medications, consultations, and diagnostic tests would alleviate the financial burden for seniors and encourage regular check-ups and preventive care.

### b) Training Healthcare Professionals in Geriatric Care

Expanding geriatric care training for general physicians, nurses, and healthcare workers can ensure that elderly patients receive specialized attention even in primary healthcare settings. Incorporating geriatric care into medical curricula would also create a larger pool of professionals equipped to handle age-related healthcare needs.

### c) Community-Based Senior Support Programs

Local communities can create support groups, transportation services, and volunteer-based systems to assist elderly individuals with healthcare needs. Community centres could host health camps, exercise classes, and educational workshops to encourage seniors to prioritize their health and well-being.

### d) Enhancing Telehealth Services for Seniors

Telemedicine platforms could be made more accessible for seniors by incorporating user-friendly interfaces, simplified instructions, and multilingual options. Furthermore, training volunteers to assist elderly individuals in navigating telehealth services could help bridge the digital divide, allowing more seniors to benefit from remote consultations.

### e) Encouraging Family Involvement and Awareness

Educating families on elderly care can help them support their elderly members in accessing healthcare. Families can encourage regular check-ups, help with medication adherence, and stay vigilant about early signs of health issues. Creating awareness among family members about the importance of emotional support for the elderly also plays a critical role in comprehensive elderly care.

Access to healthcare and geriatric services is vital for promoting health, independence, and quality of life among the elderly. While urban areas are developing resources to address the healthcare needs of seniors, barriers related to cost, accessibility, and awareness still pose significant challenges. Strengthening geriatric services through community support, family involvement, and improved healthcare infrastructure will ensure that urban elderly individuals receive the care and support they deserve. As society continues to age, investing in elderly healthcare access will be essential for building a compassionate and inclusive community where seniors can thrive with dignity and good health.

**Example 1**: Radha, a 78-year-old widow living in Bengaluru, has struggled with diabetes and hypertension for years. Her children live abroad, and she manages her daily routine independently. Radha finds it challenging to travel to the hospital every month due to her mobility issues and fears the physical strain of crowded public transportation. When her blood pressure recently spiked, her neighbour suggested a telemedicine consultation. Initially hesitant, Radha reached out to a local telemedicine platform with her daughter's help and was able to consult a doctor over video. The doctor adjusted her medication and advised her on diet changes.

Telemedicine has since become a lifeline for Radha, allowing her to manage her chronic conditions from home. Despite her initial hesitation, she now feels empowered to take control of her health and avoid exhausting trips to the hospital. This new way of accessing healthcare has greatly reduced her stress and physical discomfort, demonstrating how telemedicine can bridge healthcare gaps for elderly individuals.

**Example 2**: Ganeshan, an 82-year-old retired professor living in Chennai, has been dealing with arthritis and vision loss, making everyday tasks like grocery shopping or attending doctor's appointments challenging. His son, who lives in another city, enrolled him in a home healthcare program through a local provider that offers biweekly check-ups, physiotherapy, and even medication delivery.

Initially unfamiliar with the idea, Ganeshan was impressed by the professionalism of the healthcare team, who now visit him regularly to check his vitals and assist with exercises to manage his arthritis. The program also connected him to a specialist through teleconsultations, reducing his dependency on family or friends for transport. Ganeshan now feels a renewed sense of independence, knowing that he has reliable medical care without needing to step outside his home. Home healthcare has not only improved his physical health but also relieved his family from constant worry, making it a supportive model for elderly care.

# Part 3
# Social and Emotional Well-Being

# Loneliness and Social Isolation in Urban Settings

In urban settings, where the pace of life is fast and family structures are increasingly nuclear, elderly individuals often face loneliness and social isolation. The migration of younger generations to different cities or countries, smaller family units, and limited social interaction can leave older adults feeling isolated and disconnected from society. This isolation can significantly affect both mental and physical health, leading to issues such as depression, anxiety, and increased vulnerability to chronic illness.

Addressing loneliness and social isolation among the elderly requires a multi-layered approach, combining community efforts, family support, and individual activities that foster meaningful social connections. Programs aimed at promoting social engagement, peer support, and accessible social activities can significantly improve the quality of life for elderly individuals in urban settings.

**Understanding Loneliness and Isolation Among the Elderly**

Social isolation and loneliness are distinct but related concepts. Social isolation refers to the objective lack of social interactions or relationships, while loneliness is a subjective feeling of being alone, regardless of actual social connections. Many elderly individuals experience both, though they may not realize the impact it has on their health and well-being. The lack of regular interaction and a supportive community can lead to:

- **Mental Health Issues**: Depression, anxiety, and cognitive decline are commonly associated with prolonged loneliness.
- **Physical Health Risks**: Socially isolated individuals often exhibit higher blood pressure, weakened immune function, and an increased risk of heart disease and stroke.
- **Functional Decline**: Isolation can limit physical activity, leading to reduced mobility and muscle weakness. A lack of motivation or assistance may prevent seniors from engaging in activities that could maintain or improve their health.

In urban settings, the elderly face unique challenges that can deepen social isolation. High-rise living, busy lifestyles of family members, and the lack of a closely-knit neighbourhood structure make it difficult for seniors to foster relationships and feel engaged in their communities.

## Challenges Contributing to Loneliness in Urban Elderly Populations

Several factors contribute to the isolation and loneliness experienced by urban seniors:

### a) Distance from Family Members

In cities, younger family members often live in separate households or move away for work, leaving elderly parents on their own. With family members preoccupied with work and travel, interactions with the elderly often become infrequent. The elderly may miss regular companionship and emotional support, exacerbating feelings of loneliness.

## b) Loss of Community Ties

Unlike rural areas, where communities tend to be more tightly knit, urban areas can lack the same community connection, making it difficult for seniors to establish close relationships with neighbours. Even if seniors reside in neighbourhoods with other elderly individuals, they may lack communal spaces for interaction, such as parks or community centres.

## c) Technological Barriers

While digital tools can offer new forms of social connection, many seniors lack the skills to navigate technology effectively. This can limit their access to virtual gatherings, telehealth services, and online social groups, further isolating them from family and friends who rely on these platforms.

## d) Reduced Physical Mobility

Physical challenges can make it difficult for elderly individuals to attend social gatherings or even run daily errands, such as grocery shopping. This reduced mobility limits their ability to engage with the outside world, often confining them to their homes.

### e) Social Stigmas

For some elderly individuals, there may be a reluctance to admit feelings of loneliness or ask for help. Cultural norms may discourage expressing emotions, leading them to silently cope with loneliness rather than seek out companionship or social activities.

## Strategies for Addressing Loneliness and Building Social Connections

Addressing social isolation among the elderly requires a concerted effort across multiple areas: community, family, and personal engagement. Here are some effective strategies:

### a) Community-Based Programs and Senior Centres

Establishing community-based programs and senior centres can provide a dedicated space for elderly individuals to connect and socialize. Programs can include:

- **Recreational Activities**: Organized activities like yoga, dance classes, and arts and crafts provide social interaction and a sense of purpose.
- **Interest Groups**: Senior centres can create interest-based groups, such as gardening, music, or literature clubs, where elderly individuals can bond over shared hobbies.
- **Learning Sessions**: Workshops on topics like nutrition, technology, and mental wellness not only engage seniors but also provide practical skills.

Many urban areas, such as Chennai and Bengaluru, have introduced these programs within residential communities, offering seniors easy access to activities without extensive travel.

**b) Promoting Intergenerational Engagement**

Connecting elderly individuals with younger generations can bring joy and purpose to both groups. Schools and colleges can create volunteer programs where students spend time with the elderly, engage in conversations, or assist them with daily tasks. Programs like "Adopt a Grandparent" have shown positive effects by fostering meaningful relationships across generations, helping elderly individuals feel valued and appreciated.

**c) Leveraging Technology for Social Connection**

Technology can be a powerful tool for alleviating loneliness if made accessible to seniors. Digital literacy programs for the elderly can teach them how to use smartphones and social media, enabling them to connect with family and friends. Several initiatives can help:

- **Video Calls and Messaging Apps**: Platforms like WhatsApp, Zoom, and Skype allow for regular video calls with family, reducing the feeling of distance.
- **Social Media Groups**: Many senior-specific groups on Facebook and WhatsApp provide a space to share experiences, interests, and stories with like-minded individuals.
- **Virtual Clubs and Classes**: Online clubs and classes give seniors the opportunity to learn something new while

connecting with others, making social engagement convenient.

## d) Supportive Living Arrangements

Senior living communities and assisted living facilities often offer a built-in social environment. Facilities in urban areas like Chennai and Hyderabad are increasingly designed to promote social interaction through shared dining spaces, recreational areas, and organized events. Living arrangements that foster interaction can improve the mental and emotional well-being of elderly residents, making them feel like an integral part of a community.

## e) Creating Volunteer Networks

Volunteer networks can offer seniors companionship, practical support, and someone to talk to. Local governments and community organizations can create initiatives where trained volunteers regularly check in on elderly residents, help with errands, and engage in social activities. This approach not only supports seniors but also strengthens the sense of community within urban neighbourhoods.

## Examples of Programs Promoting Social Engagement in Urban Settings

Urban centres are beginning to recognize the importance of combating social isolation among the elderly and have implemented programs to address this issue. For example:

- **"Elderly Helpline Services"**: Many cities have set up helplines for elderly individuals that provide resources for social support, counselling, and emergency assistance. Helplines such as "Dignity Foundation" offer social engagement programs, counselling, and a "Companionship at Home" service to reduce isolation.
- **Daycare Centres and Community Groups**: Cities like Bengaluru and Chennai have introduced senior daycare centres where elderly individuals can participate in daily activities, meet friends, and receive health support. Programs like these offer structure, engagement, and social connection, which are crucial for combating loneliness.
- **Neighbourhood Groups**: Residential societies and apartment complexes sometimes organize "Seniors' Day Out" events where the elderly go on group outings, attend festivals, and celebrate birthdays together. These small gatherings create a sense of camaraderie and a feeling of belonging in the community.

## The Role of Family in Reducing Social Isolation

Family support remains essential in reducing loneliness among the elderly. Even when family members live separately, they can:
- **Encourage Regular Communication**: Making time for regular phone or video calls can provide much-needed emotional support for elderly family members.
- **Help with Technology**: Younger family members can guide elderly relatives in using technology, enabling them to connect virtually with friends and family.

- **Visit Regularly**: Occasional visits, especially during festivals or special occasions, offer companionship and help elderly individuals feel connected to family traditions.
- **Plan Family Gatherings**: Organizing get-togethers that include extended family allows elderly members to socialize, share stories, and engage in a supportive setting.

**Personal Initiatives and Activities to Combat Loneliness**

Encouraging elderly individuals to engage in activities they enjoy can help them feel fulfilled and connected. Personal activities that promote mental and emotional health include:

- **Learning New Skills**: Taking up new hobbies such as painting, knitting, or learning a new language can offer satisfaction and even open up new social circles.

- **Engaging in Spiritual or Religious Activities**: Many elderly individuals find comfort and community through religious gatherings, prayer groups, or meditation, which also provide a sense of purpose.

- **Physical Activity**: Exercise, even if limited to walking, provides both physical and mental health benefits. Joining a walking group, if available, can also provide a social outlet.

In an urban context, addressing loneliness and social isolation among the elderly requires both structural changes and community-based solutions. Building social connections for elderly individuals involves community-driven initiatives, family support, and accessible programs that encourage social engagement. By creating inclusive and senior-friendly environments, urban areas can ensure that elderly residents remain connected, fulfilled, and valued, making them integral parts of their communities.

> **Example 1**: Mr. Srinivasan, a retired 75-year-old engineer living in Chennai, had recently lost his wife and was struggling with loneliness. His son, who worked long hours, encouraged him to join a nearby senior daycare centre that organized social activities and classes. Initially reluctant, Mr. Srinivasan decided to give it a try. The centre offered activities he enjoyed, like yoga and art sessions, and gave him a chance to meet other seniors with similar interests.
>
> Over time, he found himself looking forward to these sessions, bonding with others over stories from their past and discussing books they'd read. The staff even organized group outings to temples and local cultural events, which made him feel active and socially connected again. By engaging in these activities, Mr. Srinivasan not only alleviated his loneliness but also discovered a supportive community, which transformed his outlook on aging in the city.
>
> **Example 2**: Meenakshi, an 80-year-old grandmother in Bengaluru, felt increasingly isolated as her family members, including her grandchildren, had moved abroad for work and studies. Communication was limited to the occasional phone call, and Meenakshi felt distant from her family. Her daughter suggested that she join a digital literacy program run by a local NGO. Through

this program, Meenakshi learned to use a smartphone and participate in video calls.

Once comfortable with technology, she joined a seniors' virtual book club and started making video calls with her family regularly. Her new skills allowed her to attend her granddaughter's virtual graduation ceremony, reconnecting her with family milestones.

Additionally, the book club gave her a group of friends with whom she could discuss literature and shared experiences. Learning to navigate technology gave Meenakshi both a social outlet and a renewed sense of connection with her family, reducing her loneliness significantly.

# Family Caregiving: Challenges and Responsibilities

In the rapidly evolving urban landscape of South India, where traditional family structures face the pressures of modern life, the subject of caregiving for the elderly emerges as both a responsibility and a challenge. The role of family caregivers is pivotal; they offer a profound sense of security, familiarity, and emotional support to their aging loved ones. However, the journey of caregiving can be demanding, laden with emotional, physical, and financial strains. This article explores the various facets of family caregiving, particularly the challenges faced and responsibilities undertaken by family members, within the context of urban families.

**The Cultural Significance of Family Caregiving**

Indian culture places immense value on family bonds, respect for elders, and duty towards parents. Caring for aging parents or elderly relatives is often viewed as a moral obligation, ingrained through generations of cultural and religious teachings. Terms like "Pitru Seva" (service to parents) and "Dharma" (duty) reinforce the concept that looking after one's parents is an essential responsibility, carrying spiritual merit as well. Despite these strong values, the socio-economic changes in urban society have introduced complexities that sometimes challenge these traditional expectations.

**Challenges of Family Caregiving**

The challenges faced by family caregivers can be multifaceted, often stemming from the tension between traditional expectations and modern-day realities. Below are some of the common challenges caregivers encounter.

**A. Time Constraints and Work-Life Balance**

In many urban families, both men and women are increasingly involved in professional careers, often working long hours to meet financial obligations. The lack of flexibility in work schedules makes it difficult to provide consistent care for elderly family members. Caregivers, especially those in nuclear families, find themselves stretched thin between their job responsibilities, personal lives, and caregiving duties. This can result in burnout, fatigue, and emotional strain as they struggle to balance multiple roles.

**B. Financial Strain**

Caring for an elderly family member can be financially taxing. Medical expenses, caregiving supplies, and in some cases, paid help, add to the family's expenditures. Additionally, many families may not have comprehensive health insurance coverage, leaving them to bear the brunt of high out-of-pocket medical costs. For middle-income families, this can create significant financial pressure, sometimes affecting their savings and future plans.

## C. Physical and Emotional Exhaustion

Caregiving, especially for elderly individuals with chronic illnesses or disabilities, is physically demanding. Tasks such as bathing, dressing, feeding, and managing medications require physical strength and stamina. Additionally, the emotional aspect of caregiving can be equally taxing. Watching a loved one struggle with age-related ailments, cognitive decline, or loss of independence can evoke feelings of sadness, frustration, and helplessness. Many caregivers in India report experiencing high levels of stress and anxiety, which may even lead to depression in some cases.

## D. Lack of Support and Respite Care

In traditional extended families, caregiving responsibilities could be shared among multiple family members. However, with the rise of nuclear family structures in urban societies, this support system is often lacking. The primary caregiver, usually the daughter or daughter-in-law, might be left to handle the responsibilities alone. Without adequate support or respite, caregivers may face isolation and emotional fatigue, impacting their health and well-being. Access to professional respite care services, which are limited in many Indian cities, is essential for caregivers to have a break and recharge.

## E. Navigating Healthcare and Legal Systems

The healthcare needs of the elderly can be complex, involving multiple specialists, hospital visits, and long-term medications.

Family caregivers often bear the responsibility of coordinating medical appointments, managing prescriptions, and making healthcare decisions. Navigating the healthcare system can be overwhelming, particularly with the fragmented nature of medical services in urban India. Additionally, legal responsibilities—such as power of attorney, managing finances, and ensuring compliance with government schemes for the elderly—pose another layer of complexity.

### F. Social Stigma and Isolation

In Indian society, especially in conservative families, hiring external help for caregiving may carry a social stigma. Some families perceive it as a deviation from traditional values, where taking care of elders is seen as a family duty. This can lead to isolation for the primary caregiver, who may feel compelled to shoulder the responsibility alone to avoid societal judgment. This isolation is exacerbated for caregivers who, due to the demands of caregiving, may withdraw from their social networks.

### Responsibilities of Family Caregivers

Despite the challenges, family caregivers bear profound responsibilities. Their role extends beyond meeting physical needs; they are often the primary source of emotional support and companionship for the elderly. Here are some key responsibilities that family caregivers typically manage.

## A. Ensuring Physical Care and Safety

The primary responsibility of family caregivers is to meet the physical needs of the elderly. This includes tasks such as bathing, dressing, feeding, and administering medications. For seniors with mobility issues, caregivers need to take precautions to prevent falls and injuries, often requiring modifications in the home environment to enhance safety. They may also arrange for medical equipment such as wheelchairs, walkers, or oxygen tanks to support their loved one's daily functioning.

## B. Providing Emotional Support and Companionship

One of the most critical aspects of caregiving is offering emotional support. Loneliness and isolation are common among the elderly, particularly in urban environments where social interactions are limited. Family caregivers provide companionship, engage in meaningful conversations, and encourage activities that keep the elderly mentally stimulated. By fostering a warm, empathetic environment, caregivers help improve the mental well-being of their loved ones.

## C. Managing Healthcare Needs

From scheduling doctor's appointments to overseeing medication schedules, family caregivers play an active role in managing the healthcare needs of the elderly. They must stay informed about the medical condition of their loved ones, monitor symptoms, and promptly seek medical attention if necessary. In cases of chronic illness, caregivers often become well-versed in specific treatments, medications, and therapies, acting as an intermediary between healthcare providers and the elderly.

## D. Coordinating Social and Recreational Activities

Engaging the elderly in social and recreational activities is essential for their mental and emotional well-being. Family caregivers in South India often organize social outings, religious visits, or gatherings with relatives to ensure that their loved ones stay connected with family and community. For many elderly individuals, religious practices are a significant source of comfort; caregivers might facilitate visits to temples or arrange for participation in festivals, helping the elderly maintain a sense of continuity with their cultural roots.

## E. Overseeing Financial Matters

Managing finances is a crucial responsibility, especially for elderly family members who may be financially dependent or unable to handle their finances due to cognitive decline. Caregivers often take charge of paying bills, managing bank accounts, and ensuring timely access to pension funds or retirement savings. This role requires a great deal of trust and integrity, as well as familiarity with financial planning, tax regulations, and government schemes designed to benefit senior citizens.

## F. Advocacy and Decision-Making

Family caregivers serve as advocates, representing the elderly in decisions related to healthcare, living arrangements, and end-of-life planning. Making decisions on behalf of an aging family member requires sensitivity, as caregivers must balance the autonomy and preferences of the elderly with their safety and well-being. In cases where the elderly suffer from dementia or cognitive impairment, caregivers may also be responsible for arranging legal documents such as power of attorney and wills, ensuring that decisions align with their loved one's wishes.

**Coping Mechanisms for Caregivers**

To manage the challenges of caregiving, family caregivers need effective coping mechanisms. Here are some strategies that can help mitigate the stress associated with caregiving:

**A. Building a Support Network**

Connecting with other family members, friends, or support groups can provide emotional relief and practical advice. Support networks offer a platform to share experiences, gain encouragement, and find camaraderie among others who understand the challenges of caregiving.

**B. Seeking Respite Care**

Temporary respite care, whether provided by professional caregivers or family members, is essential for maintaining the caregiver's well-being. It offers caregivers a much-needed break to rest and rejuvenate, helping them return to their duties with renewed energy.

## C. Practicing Self-Care

Caregivers must prioritize their physical and mental health by incorporating exercise, proper nutrition, and adequate rest into their routine. Engaging in activities such as meditation, hobbies, or social outings can help caregivers relieve stress and maintain a positive outlook.

## D. Utilizing Community Resources

Many urban centres have elder-care facilities, NGOs, and support services designed to assist caregivers. These resources offer valuable assistance, from home healthcare services to counselling sessions, that can ease the burden on family caregivers.

Family caregiving is an indispensable yet complex role within urban families, embodying a blend of cultural responsibility and evolving practical challenges. Despite the emotional, physical, and financial burdens, the caregiving journey can be immensely fulfilling, providing opportunities for deeper bonds and meaningful connections.

By addressing the challenges and embracing their responsibilities, caregivers can help ensure that their elderly loved ones live with dignity, comfort, and love, even in their twilight years. The caregiving experience is thus a delicate balance—one that requires compassion, resilience, and community support. As society recognizes the vital role of family caregivers, increased awareness and resources can help make this responsibility more sustainable, benefiting both caregivers and the elderly.

**Example 1: Balancing Work and Caregiving Responsibilities**

Shanti, a 45-year-old software engineer in Chennai, lives with her husband, two school-aged children, and her 78-year-old mother, Kamala. Shanti's mother was recently diagnosed with Parkinson's disease, and her condition requires regular medication, assistance with mobility, and monitoring. Shanti has taken on the role of her mother's primary caregiver, but the demands of her full-time job and responsibilities as a parent make this role challenging.

**Challenges and Responsibilities**

Every morning, Shanti wakes up early to help her mother with her daily routine—she assists with bathing, prepares breakfast, and makes sure her mother's medications are taken on time. The physical toll of lifting and moving her mother, coupled with the emotional stress of seeing her health decline, affects Shanti's own well-being. Despite her best efforts, Shanti often feels guilty for not being able to spend as much time with her children or take on additional projects at work.

To cope, Shanti reaches out to a local support group for caregivers in Chennai, which offers her both practical advice and emotional support. She also arranges for a part-time caregiver to assist her mother in the afternoons while she's at work. However, Shanti finds it challenging to navigate the stigma around hiring external help, as some family members feel that caregiving should be a "family responsibility."

This example illustrates how the traditional expectations of family caregiving can clash with the demands of modern work life, making it difficult for caregivers to strike a balance. Shanti's journey underscores the need for understanding within the family and the importance of support systems for urban caregivers.

**Example 2: Navigating Healthcare and Social Stigma in End-of-Life Care**

Ravi, a 52-year-old businessman in Bangalore, is caring for his 84-year-old father, Narayan, who is in the advanced stages of dementia. Narayan requires 24/7 care, as he often forgets who and where he is, becomes agitated at night, and needs assistance with all basic activities. Ravi's family is supportive, but they lack the expertise to manage Narayan's complex needs.

**Challenges and Responsibilities**

Initially, Ravi and his wife tried to manage Narayan's care on their own, but the intensity of the role began affecting their physical and mental health. With the lack of in-home healthcare services specifically designed for dementia patients in their neighbourhood, Ravi explored the idea of moving his father to a professional care facility that specialized in dementia care. However, he faced strong opposition from extended family members, who believed that sending an elder to a care facility was disrespectful and went against their family values.

After discussing it with his immediate family, Ravi decided to consult with a geriatric care manager who provided insights into dementia care and helped facilitate a compromise. Ravi arranged for in-home visits by trained dementia care specialists, allowing his father to stay at home while receiving the necessary medical attention. This decision involved a significant financial commitment, but Ravi found it essential to ensure his father's well-being.

Through this experience, Ravi realized the challenges posed by the stigma around elder care facilities. His journey illustrates the delicate balance between honouring cultural values and making practical decisions that prioritize the health and dignity of the elderly. Ravi's proactive approach to seeking specialized care highlights the importance of resources and education around elder care, particularly for conditions that require specialized treatment

# Intergenerational Relationships in South Indian Families

Intergenerational relationships—connections between different age groups within families—play a crucial role in the traditional structure of households. Rooted in centuries-old customs, these bonds provide support, stability, and guidance, especially in the context of elder care. In Indian families, respect for elders and a sense of duty toward the family are intrinsic values, shaping the dynamics between generations. However, as families evolve and societal norms change, these relationships face both challenges and transformations. This section delves into the cultural, social, and emotional aspects of intergenerational relationships in families, examining how these connections impact elderly care and overall family cohesion.

**Cultural Foundations of Intergenerational Bonds**

Indian culture places immense emphasis on the family as a fundamental social unit. Families are often multigenerational, with grandparents, parents, and children living together or in close proximity. The value of respect for elders is instilled from a young age, influenced by religious beliefs and cultural narratives that honour the wisdom and life experiences of older generations.

Traditions such as joint family celebrations, festival rituals, and religious ceremonies allow family members to come together and reinforce familial ties. Elders are viewed as custodians of cultural heritage, sharing stories, folk wisdom, and values that younger generations carry forward. Such cultural settings promote interdependence and allow family members to stay connected, with grandparents often playing a significant role in nurturing young children and passing down traditions.

**Roles and Responsibilities Across Generations**

Intergenerational relationships in India are often defined by specific roles and responsibilities. Elders are typically seen as guides and counsellors, providing emotional support and advice in family decisions. This guidance extends to financial planning, career choices, and even marriage decisions, as their experiences are deemed invaluable. Younger generations, in turn, have traditionally taken on the role of caregivers for their aging parents and grandparents. The concept of *seva* (service) to elders is culturally significant, rooted in the belief that looking after one's parents is not just a moral duty but also a path to spiritual fulfilment. This sense of responsibility extends to ensuring physical, financial, and emotional well-being for the elderly family members, with children often prioritizing their parents' needs over their own aspirations.

**Emotional Benefits of Intergenerational Bonds**

The emotional benefits of intergenerational relationships in families are profound. For the elderly, close relationships with younger family members can provide a sense of purpose, security, and fulfilment. Knowing that they are cherished and needed by the family can positively affect their mental health and overall well-being. They often find joy and satisfaction in participating in their grandchildren's lives, from celebrating milestones to helping with schoolwork, which gives them a feeling of continued relevance and vitality.

Younger generations, too, benefit emotionally from these bonds. Elders offer a sense of stability and provide a safe environment for children to discuss their fears, challenges, and aspirations. Stories of resilience and family history shared by grandparents or older family members can help the younger generation gain perspective and resilience, especially in times of stress. These relationships often create a powerful emotional support system within the family, building resilience across generations.

## Challenges in Modern Intergenerational Relationships

Despite the strong foundation of intergenerational ties, these relationships face significant challenges due to changing societal structures and values. Urbanization, increased mobility, and changing economic realities have led to smaller nuclear families and a decline in traditional joint-family systems. Many young professionals move to urban centres or abroad for better job opportunities, leaving behind aging parents who may feel isolated or neglected.

Additionally, generational differences in values, lifestyle choices, and communication styles can sometimes create friction. Younger generations may view traditional beliefs as restrictive, while older generations may struggle to understand the more liberal attitudes of today's youth. In some cases, the presence of technology and a fast-paced lifestyle can cause younger people to spend less time interacting meaningfully with their elders, leading to a sense of disconnect.

**Adaptation and Transformation of Intergenerational Bonds**

South Indian families are finding ways to adapt to these changing dynamics without losing the essence of intergenerational relationships. One notable trend is the increasing acceptance of digital communication to bridge physical distances. Video calls, social media, and messaging apps allow families to stay connected, share updates, and celebrate moments together, even if they are geographically separated.

Families are also making efforts to facilitate intergenerational interaction during special occasions, vacations, or festivals, often organizing family gatherings that bring together multiple generations. Such events provide an opportunity for elders to connect with younger family members in a relaxed and celebratory atmosphere, strengthening emotional bonds despite physical distances.

Moreover, some families are exploring formal elder care options, like senior living communities, while maintaining close ties with their elders. This hybrid approach allows the elderly to receive professional care while their family members remain involved, visiting regularly and participating in the care planning. This approach acknowledges the practical needs of modern life while respecting traditional values of familial duty and connection.

## Economic Implications on Intergenerational Relationships

Economic factors significantly influence intergenerational relationships in families. Financial security is a major concern for many elderly individuals, who may rely on their children for financial support. Traditionally, children were expected to take care of their parents in their old age, but economic pressures and the rising cost of living are reshaping these expectations. Dual-income households, the increased cost of childcare, and financial responsibilities to one's own children can make it challenging for younger generations to provide the same level of support as before.

This financial strain can sometimes create tension within families. Some elderly parents may feel disappointed if they perceive a lack of support, while younger generations may experience guilt or frustration. However, families are increasingly discussing and planning for financial stability, encouraging elders to invest in pensions, insurance, and other retirement plans. This proactive financial planning allows for greater independence and lessens the financial burden on the younger generation.

## Role of Religion and Spirituality in Strengthening Bonds

Religion and spirituality are deeply woven into the fabric of Indian family life, and they play a key role in strengthening intergenerational bonds. Regular religious observances, prayers, and visits to temples are often communal activities that bring family members together. Elders serve as custodians of religious practices, teaching younger generations about rituals, values, and spiritual beliefs.

Spirituality also helps the family to navigate the emotional challenges of caregiving, aging, and end-of-life issues. For example, during illness or bereavement, family members turn to faith for solace and resilience. These shared spiritual experiences can bring family members closer, allowing them to support one another emotionally and spiritually.

**Impact of Changing Gender Roles on Intergenerational Dynamics**

Traditionally, caregiving responsibilities within families have largely fallen on women, who are expected to care for aging parents, in-laws, and children. However, with more women pursuing higher education and careers, these roles are shifting. Sons are now taking on caregiving responsibilities more often, and caregiving tasks are sometimes shared more equally between spouses. This shift can create both opportunities and challenges for intergenerational relationships. On one hand, sharing caregiving duties can strengthen relationships between family members by fostering mutual understanding and cooperation. On the other, generational expectations may clash with modern gender roles, with some elders struggling to accept new norms where daughters or daughters-in-law might not be primary caregivers.

**The Role of Education in Shaping Intergenerational Relationships**

Education plays a transformative role in shaping attitudes toward elderly care and intergenerational relationships. Younger generations are increasingly exposed to diverse ideas and lifestyles through formal education, media, and travel, which can influence how they perceive their roles within the family. Education encourages more open communication, empathy, and respect for individual preferences, fostering healthier and more understanding intergenerational relationships.

For instance, educated family members are more likely to explore alternative care options, advocate for the rights of elderly family members, and approach caregiving with a more informed and compassionate outlook. Educational exposure also increases awareness about mental health, encouraging more sensitive and patient interactions with elderly family members, especially those dealing with age-related cognitive decline.

**Future of Intergenerational Relationships in South India**

The future of intergenerational relationships holds both challenges and possibilities. As traditional family structures evolve, there is a need to balance respect for cultural values with the realities of modern life. Families are likely to continue adapting to changes by embracing flexible approaches to caregiving and connection, while maintaining the essence of intergenerational respect and duty.

There is also a growing trend of integrating technology into family life, with the younger generation teaching their elders to use smartphones, apps, and other digital tools to stay connected. This mutual sharing of knowledge fosters respect and understanding, bridging generational gaps. Additionally, awareness of mental health and the need for emotional well-being are reshaping how families approach intergenerational communication, caregiving, and conflict resolution.

In summary, intergenerational relationships families are evolving in response to changing social, economic, and cultural factors. While the challenges are real, the resilience of these relationships lies in their adaptability. As families continue to honour traditional values while embracing modern realities, they create an enduring legacy of love, respect, and mutual support across generations.

---

**Example 1: The Rao Family – Bridging Physical Distance Through Digital Bonds**

**Family Structure and Background:** The Rao family consists of 72-year-old Saroja and her husband Rajendra, who live in Chennai. Their two children, Vishal and Kavya, are both professionals who have moved abroad for career opportunities. Vishal, the elder son, works as an IT consultant in the United States, and Kavya is a doctor in the United Kingdom. The Raos initially lived in a joint family setting, but as the children moved abroad, they felt the impact of distance keenly, especially regarding the physical separation from their grandchildren.

**Intergenerational Dynamics and Challenges:** Saroja and Rajendra cherish their grandchildren and feel deeply connected to them, but the geographical separation has made regular, in-person interaction difficult. The grandparents miss participating in their grandchildren's milestones, while the grandchildren lack direct exposure to culture and family traditions. Saroja often worries that her grandchildren will not understand or appreciate their roots without the chance to experience festivals, customs, and traditional values firsthand.

**Adaptations and Strengthening the Bond:** Understanding the impact of distance, Vishal and Kavya made efforts to integrate technology into their family's daily life. They set up video calls multiple times a week, during which Saroja tells her grandchildren stories about their culture, often incorporating folk tales, mythological narratives, and festival customs. On special occasions, like Diwali or Pongal, Vishal and Kavya arrange virtual gatherings, where the children dress in traditional attire, and Saroja explains each ritual and the values it represents.

Saroja and Rajendra also adapted by learning how to use smartphones, video call platforms, and messaging apps. Initially resistant to technology, Saroja now enjoys sending "good morning" messages with blessings to her family, sharing her garden updates, and sending voice notes with bedtime stories for her grandchildren. This digital bridge has not only helped them stay connected but has also strengthened the emotional bond between generations, despite the physical distance.

**Outcome:** The Raos have successfully adapted to modern technology to maintain close intergenerational relationships. Although they may not be physically present, Saroja and Rajendra feel involved in their grandchildren's lives, passing down cultural wisdom and love through virtual means. The grandchildren, in turn, grow up with a deep sense of their heritage, despite being raised far from their roots.

**Example 2: The Menon Family – Navigating Caregiving and Generational Expectations**

**Family Structure and Background:** The Menon family lives in Bangalore and comprises three generations under one roof: 65-year-old Lakshmi and her husband Natarajan, their son Ravi (age 40), Ravi's wife Deepa, and their two children, Ananya and Aarav, aged 12 and 8. Lakshmi and Natarajan are retired, with Natarajan experiencing mobility issues due to arthritis, which has gradually increased his dependence on family members.

**Intergenerational Dynamics and Challenges:** As the family's oldest members, Lakshmi and Natarajan expect a degree of respect and obedience from younger generations, including their son and daughter-in-law. They grew up in a traditional setting where caregiving was mainly a woman's duty, and they find it difficult to understand why Deepa, who works as a software engineer, cannot devote more time to their care. This expectation puts strain on Deepa, who, while respectful of her in-laws, also values her career and feels that caregiving responsibilities should be shared.

Ravi, balancing responsibilities to his parents, wife, and children, finds himself in a challenging position. He respects his parents' wishes but also wants to support Deepa's career ambitions. The different generational expectations regarding caregiving lead to occasional conflicts and misunderstandings within the family.

**Adaptations and Compromise:** After several family discussions, they reach a compromise. To support Natarajan's mobility issues, Ravi and Deepa hire a part-time caregiver who assists with his physical needs during the day. Deepa, understanding the importance of cultural traditions, sets aside specific weekends to accompany Lakshmi and Natarajan to temple visits or family gatherings, honouring their values and participating in rituals that strengthen family ties.

The children, Ananya and Aarav, are encouraged to spend time with their grandparents daily, listening to their stories or helping with small tasks around the house. Lakshmi starts teaching Ananya how to cook traditional dishes, explaining the history behind each recipe and its significance to South Indian culture. This arrangement creates a meaningful connection between the younger and older generations, where the children learn and participate in their heritage while the grandparents feel valued and included.

**Outcome:** The Menons have embraced a balanced approach to caregiving, respecting Lakshmi and Natarajan's cultural expectations while also addressing the realities of a dual-income household. This adjustment fosters an environment of mutual respect and understanding. By sharing responsibilities and encouraging interaction between the children and their grandparents, the family nurtures a strong, multi-dimensional bond, allowing each generation to feel both supported and respected.

# The Role of Faith & Spirituality in Aging

As individuals age, they often undergo profound transformations, seeking deeper meanings and connections in life. In India, faith and spirituality are integral to this journey, shaping perspectives on aging, wellness, and mortality. This article delves into the role of faith and spirituality in the lives of the elderly, highlighting how these elements provide comfort, resilience, and a sense of community. From traditional practices to modern spiritual adaptations, the role of spirituality in aging is deeply woven into the fabric of society.

**Faith and Aging**

The aging process involves navigating physical, emotional, and social changes. As the body slows down and traditional roles shift, many find themselves contemplating existential questions about purpose, fulfilment, and life's legacy. For the elderly, faith and spirituality are often pillars of support, helping them cope with life's transitions. Studies show that spirituality can contribute to improved psychological health, emotional stability, and resilience among the elderly. In India, these benefits are evident in the daily lives of seniors, who frequently turn to spiritual practices for guidance and strength.

Faith and spirituality encompass a diverse range of beliefs and practices rooted in Hinduism, Islam, Christianity, Jainism, and other spiritual paths. These religions offer structured rituals and teachings that aid seniors in maintaining a sense of purpose, comfort, and community as they age. Faith traditions also provide unique perspectives on aging and death, encouraging acceptance and peace, which are invaluable during one's twilight years.

**Traditional Beliefs and Cultural Values**

Aging is traditionally viewed with reverence and respect, with elderly members considered wise and esteemed. Cultural values rooted in spirituality emphasize gratitude, respect, and the idea of "karmic balance," where actions in life are believed to influence one's later years. This spiritual understanding instils a sense of purpose and moral responsibility, allowing seniors to view aging as a sacred journey rather than merely a biological process. For instance, Hinduism emphasizes the "ashrama" system, categorizing life into four stages: Brahmacharya (student life), Grihastha (householder life), Vanaprastha (retired life), and Sannyasa (renunciation). For the elderly, the Vanaprastha and Sannyasa stages encourage individuals to withdraw from material pursuits, focusing instead on self-reflection, meditation, and spiritual fulfilment. Similarly, Islamic practices encourage elderly Muslims to seek closeness to Allah through prayer and charitable deeds, while Christianity emphasizes finding peace and strength through faith and service. These traditional values and beliefs create a guiding framework for aging gracefully.

**Spiritual Practices and Their Impact on Well-being**

Many seniors in turn to practices like meditation, prayer, and chanting as ways to maintain spiritual health. These practices offer more than mere ritualistic value—they are therapeutic tools that aid in calming the mind, promoting mental clarity, and reducing anxiety. Studies have shown that spiritual practices can help lower stress, improve mood, and even strengthen the immune system, contributing to overall well-being.

1. **Meditation and Yoga**: Originating from Hinduism and Buddhism, meditation and yoga are not merely fitness routines but spiritual exercises for mental clarity and inner peace. Regular practice can help seniors manage physical discomfort and emotional stress, while also fostering a sense of connection with the divine. Many senior centres and communities now offer accessible yoga and meditation sessions specifically tailored for the elderly, supporting both physical and spiritual health.

2. **Pilgrimages and Religious Tourism**: For many seniors, pilgrimages to sacred places such as Tirupati, Sabarimala, or Velankanni become significant spiritual goals. These journeys are not merely physical trips but represent deeply meaningful spiritual milestones.

    Despite physical limitations, elderly individuals often undertake such journeys with zeal, viewing them as an essential part of life's closure. Religious tourism has also seen a rise, with families arranging visits to temples and religious sites to fulfil the wishes of their elderly loved ones.

3. **Prayer and Rituals**: Daily prayer and rituals are essential in many households, where traditions like lighting oil lamps, reciting slokas (chants), and offering prayers continue across generations. For elderly individuals, these rituals offer stability and a sense of routine. They are reminders of their role within the family and serve as quiet moments of connection with the divine. The ritualistic aspects bring comfort and familiarity, providing emotional support through the security of established customs.

## Role of Community and Family Support in Spirituality

In Indian culture, spirituality and faith are communal experiences, often practiced within family settings. Family gatherings, festival celebrations, and religious events allow elderly individuals to share their faith with loved ones, fostering a sense of belonging and purpose. The role of family in supporting elderly spirituality cannot be overstated. It is common to see younger generations accompanying their elders to temples, religious events, and ceremonies, providing both practical assistance and emotional companionship.

Many communities also organize satsangs (spiritual gatherings), discourses, and study groups that encourage seniors to share experiences, reflect on spiritual teachings, and find companionship among peers. These gatherings foster social interaction and create a supportive community, helping to alleviate loneliness and isolation among the elderly. With increased migration and nuclear family structures, senior citizens' associations, religious institutions, and social groups are increasingly filling this role, offering spiritual programs tailored to the elderly.

**Coping with Loss, Grief, and Loneliness through Faith**

The aging process inevitably brings experiences of loss—whether it be the loss of a spouse, friends, or physical abilities. For many, these losses can lead to feelings of loneliness, depression, or anxiety. Spirituality offers a way to process and accept these losses, providing comfort through the belief in a higher power and the idea of an afterlife or reincarnation.

In Hinduism, the belief in the cycle of birth and rebirth can be particularly comforting, as it allows seniors to view death as a continuation rather than an end. Similarly, Christian and Islamic teachings offer the hope of an eternal afterlife, encouraging the elderly to find peace with mortality.

Such beliefs provide a framework for understanding loss, helping individuals cope with grief through spiritual acceptance and trust in a greater divine plan.

Many elderly individuals also find solace in bhajans (devotional songs), religious readings, and discussions with spiritual leaders, who offer guidance and counsel. Temples, churches, and mosques often serve as safe spaces for those struggling with grief, offering emotional support through shared beliefs and rituals.

## Spirituality and Healthcare: Integrating Faith with Modern Medicine

In recent years, there has been a growing awareness of the importance of spirituality in healthcare, particularly in geriatric care. Healthcare providers in increasingly recognize the role of faith in the emotional and psychological well-being of elderly patients. Integrating spirituality into healthcare can be beneficial in palliative care settings, where providing comfort and dignity is paramount. Spiritual counselling, chaplaincy services, and support for religious practices within hospitals are becoming more common, catering to the spiritual needs of elderly patients.

For many elderly patients, discussing their spiritual beliefs with healthcare providers can be empowering, giving them a sense of agency and fulfilment. Research has shown that patients who receive spiritual support are often more satisfied with their care and experience better overall well-being. Integrating spirituality in healthcare allows for a holistic approach that respects the cultural and spiritual identity of seniors, ultimately enhancing the quality of geriatric care.

## Embracing the Journey of Aging with Faith

Faith and spirituality are inseparable from the aging experience in India, offering a path of peace, strength, and resilience for elderly individuals. By engaging in spiritual practices, participating in communal rituals, and drawing support from their families and communities, seniors can navigate the challenges of aging with grace. The role of faith goes beyond religious rituals; it is a source of inner peace, acceptance, and purpose that transforms the aging process from a time of decline into a sacred phase of life.

For seniors, aging is not merely a biological phenomenon but a spiritual journey, where faith provides the light and comfort to navigate its complexities. This holistic approach encourages a graceful acceptance of life's transitions, helping the elderly find fulfilment, dignity, and peace in their later years. As society continues to evolve, the integration of faith, family, and community will remain crucial in honouring and supporting its elderly members. Through these deep-rooted spiritual traditions, the elderly are empowered to embrace the journey of aging as one of wisdom, resilience, and spiritual growth.

**Example 1. The Devout Pilgrimage of Subramaniam Iyer**

Subramaniam Iyer, a retired schoolteacher in his early 70s from Tamil Nadu, had always dreamed of visiting the four *Char Dham* pilgrimage sites in India but put off this aspiration to raise his family. When he finally retired, his health started to decline, and he began facing challenges with mobility. His family suggested he focus on nearby temples, but his deep-rooted faith inspired him to undertake at least the nearby pilgrimages, especially to temples such as Rameshwaram, Kanyakumari, and Tirupati.

With the support of his children and fellow elderly members of his temple community, Subramaniam embarked on a spiritual journey. The pilgrimage became not just a physical journey but also an emotional one, where each temple visit allowed him to reflect on his life, express gratitude, and seek forgiveness. This experience gave him a sense of accomplishment and peace, fulfilling a lifetime spiritual goal. The journey also strengthened his faith, allowing him to accept the natural process of aging gracefully and find solace in his spiritual practices.

This pilgrimage experience is common among many elderly individuals in India who see such journeys as a means of spiritual fulfilment, aiding them in preparing for the later stages of life with peace and contentment.

**Example 2. Bhajan Mandalis and Community for Lakshmi Ammal**

Lakshmi Ammal, an 82-year-old widow from Kerala, found her greatest source of joy and solace in weekly *bhajan mandalis* (devotional singing groups) organized at her local temple. After her husband passed away, Lakshmi experienced bouts of loneliness and anxiety, worsened by her children moving to different cities. Initially, she felt isolated and missed the companionship she shared with her husband.

A friend from her temple invited her to join a bhajan group where elderly women gathered to sing devotional songs, share stories from the *Bhagavad Gita*, and discuss spiritual insights. Over time, these weekly gatherings became her spiritual sanctuary and a social lifeline. The songs and chants brought her peace, while the companionship provided emotional support. Sharing her thoughts and reflections with others gave her a renewed sense of purpose and connectedness.

The bhajan mandali not only helped Lakshmi find comfort in her faith but also in her community, providing her with a space to express herself, alleviate loneliness, and form a close-knit social circle of fellow devotees. This spiritual community became a crucial part of her well-being, offering her strength, joy, and a sense of belonging during her later years.

# Cultural Practices and Rituals Surrounding Aging and Death

India is home to a plethora of cultural traditions, enriched by centuries of religious, linguistic, and community influences. For many families, cultural practices surrounding aging and death remain deeply embedded in daily life, offering guidance, comfort, and continuity in times of change. These traditions are not merely ceremonial but form a way to cope with and respect the process of aging and the inevitability of death. In urban settings, where lifestyle transformations are fast-paced and family structures are shifting, these age-old customs hold significant meaning, balancing the modern with the traditional.

Aging is often perceived as a progression toward wisdom, with elders seen as spiritual guides and repositories of family knowledge. Unlike in some cultures where aging might be met with apprehension, here, growing old is usually seen as a phase of fulfilment, when one has completed many of life's responsibilities and transitions into a role of mentorship and spiritual reflection. This section explores how these cultural views impact the way families approach aging and death, and how these rituals, though evolving, continue to provide structure and meaning.

## Aging in South Indian Culture

Respect for elders is a cornerstone of family values. Across communities, elders are honoured for their life experience, and their opinions are held in high regard, especially in family matters. Traditionally, they play a central role in guiding the younger generations and preserving cultural and religious practices. This reverence goes beyond social courtesy; it involves a structured system where elders serve as advisors, contributing to family decisions and setting moral standards. As one reaches advanced age, there is often a conscious focus on spiritual and moral growth, with increased involvement in religious practices and community service. In joint families, elders are integral to the family's daily functioning, often helping raise grandchildren and leading prayers. However, the rise of nuclear families in urban areas has transformed these dynamics. Elders are less frequently in close physical proximity to their families, often living independently or in senior living communities. This shift challenges traditional caregiving roles, sometimes creating a disconnect between generations. Despite these changes, many families strive to maintain respect for the elderly, even as caregiving responsibilities and family structures evolve.

## Cultural Practices for Elderly Care

For many elders, daily rituals and spiritual practices are essential parts of life. These routines, which often include morning prayers, temple visits, and recitation of sacred texts, provide a source of peace and a structured rhythm to the day. As physical and social capabilities may wane with age, these rituals offer emotional stability and a sense of purpose. Families often ensure that elders have access to the means to perform these rituals, such as a home altar or transportation to a temple, respecting their need for continuity in spiritual life.

Traditional healthcare practices, such as Ayurveda and Siddha, are commonly used alongside modern medicine to support the elderly's health. These practices emphasize balance, preventive care, and the use of natural remedies tailored to individual constitutions. They play a role not only in physical well-being but also in the elder's psychological comfort, as these are the methods they have grown up with. Regular oil massages, herbal treatments, and dietary practices align with these traditions and are often overseen by family members, underscoring the holistic approach to aging.

Milestone celebrations, like the *Sashtiabthapoorthi* (60th birthday), emphasize gratitude for longevity and life accomplishments. Families gather to honour elders with a ceremonial renewal of vows, symbolizing their continued role within the family and society. These events are more than celebrations; they act as rites of passage, reaffirming familial bonds and reinforcing the elder's valued position within the family structure.

**Rituals Surrounding Death and Dying**

Death, in Indian culture, is viewed as a part of the soul's journey rather than a final end. Hindu, Jain, and Buddhist communities, in particular, emphasize the cyclic nature of life (samsara) and believe in the continuity of the soul. This belief influences a compassionate and accepting approach to death, where preparations for one's passing are approached with an attitude of peace and dignity. Elderly individuals, especially those who sense their time nearing, often engage more deeply in spiritual preparation, reading religious texts or reflecting on life's purpose. Many embark on pilgrimages or visit sacred sites, seeking to cleanse their spirit and embrace life's completion with grace.

When death nears, families perform rituals to comfort the dying and ease their transition. In Hindu families, these rituals might include placing sacred basil (*Tulasi*) water on the person's lips, chanting prayers, and gathering loved ones around, creating a supportive environment. This compassionate practice emphasizes the significance of community in the final moments and ensures that the person feels cared for and honoured until the end.

**Post-Death Rituals and the Role of the Family**

After death, the family embarks on a series of rituals that provide structure and meaning during grief. Funeral customs vary among communities; Hindus typically perform cremations, while Christians and Muslims follow burial practices, each with distinct rites and symbolism. Hindu funerals are often elaborate, involving mantras, offerings, and ceremonial washing, signifying a respectful release of the body while acknowledging the soul's journey.

In Christian families, prayer services and masses are held, offering collective support and faith-based comfort, while Muslim families observe *Janaza*, a funeral prayer, and burial rituals that underscore humility and equality before God.

Following the funeral, the family observes a mourning period, where activities like *Shraadha* (a Hindu ritual) and *Thithi* (annual remembrance) are performed to honour the deceased. The family offers food and prayers, believing it nourishes the soul in the afterlife. These practices reinforce the familial bond, as members come together to uphold the memory of the deceased, finding solace in these structured customs. Mourning rituals are not solely for the departed; they provide emotional closure for the family, allowing them to express grief and, ultimately, regain normalcy.

The mourning period often culminates in a ceremony that symbolizes the family's readiness to resume daily life. The observance of these customs varies; in urban settings, families sometimes abbreviate rituals to accommodate work schedules and modern lifestyle constraints. Yet, even in these adapted forms, the rituals offer continuity and emotional comfort, grounding family members in a shared heritage.

**The Impact of Faith and Spirituality**

Religion deeply shapes attitudes toward aging and death in Indian communities. Hindu philosophy, with its emphasis on karma (action) and moksha (liberation), provides a framework that encourages elders to accept life's end as part of a larger cosmic cycle. Similarly, Christians draw comfort from beliefs in eternal life, while Muslims anticipate reunion with God. Such beliefs guide families in their approach to caregiving and bereavement, making faith an essential pillar in dealing with aging and loss.

Religious communities also play a vital role. Temples, churches, and mosques provide elderly members with a sense of belonging and solace, reinforcing the idea of collective caregiving. Family members may accompany elders to places of worship, and, in turn, the elderly participate in religious events that strengthen communal bonds. As urbanization shifts the family structure, religious gatherings help bridge the gap, providing the elderly with a source of purpose and connection.

**Modern Challenges and Adaptations**

While many families strive to uphold traditions, urban lifestyles often necessitate adaptations. Rituals are sometimes simplified or condensed to fit into a busy schedule, and many of the younger generation, view religious practices with a more flexible approach, blending them with modern values. For example, virtual meetings for death anniversaries, online prayer groups, and live-streamed funeral services have become common, especially post-pandemic, allowing family members spread across cities to participate in rituals together. Technology serves as a bridge, helping families maintain traditions, even if from a distance.

The rising awareness of mental health has also begun to influence family practices. In urban areas, families increasingly seek counselling and grief support, breaking the stigma around mental health in the context of loss. This change marks a significant shift, reflecting a growing acceptance of holistic approaches that incorporate both traditional practices and modern psychological support.

The cultural practices and rituals surrounding aging and death in South India offer much more than ceremony; they provide a framework of respect, continuity, and emotional resilience. While urbanization and modern influences present challenges to these traditions, many families continue to honour these practices as a link to their heritage. For younger generations, understanding these rituals not only fosters respect for the past but also preserves the values of empathy and community, which are essential in any era. In honouring the aging and remembering the deceased, these rituals enrich lives and offer strength, embodying the resilience and adaptability of the culture.

> **Example 1:** *Sashtiabthapoorthi* **- Celebrating the Milestone of 60 Years**
>
> Ravi and Lakshmi, a couple living in Chennai, have recently celebrated *Sashtiabthapoorthi*, a traditional Hindu ceremony marking a person's 60th birthday. This ritual, often held in Tamil Brahmin families, is not merely a birthday celebration; it signifies a rebirth and a renewed marital union in honour of having reached an important life milestone. In Ravi's family, elders and extended family gathered to witness the couple renew their vows in a formal wedding ceremony, which symbolizes respect for life, health, and marital companionship.
>
> In preparation, Lakshmi's family organized a *homam* (fire ritual) at a nearby temple, led by a family priest who guided them through

chants and prayers for prosperity, health, and longevity. As part of the ceremony, Ravi received blessings from each family member, symbolizing the transfer of familial support as he embraced this new phase of life.

Their children, who live in other cities, managed to attend the ceremony virtually, participating in the blessings through a video call. Even with some modifications due to distance, the family was able to uphold this tradition. The ceremony left a lasting impression on Ravi's grandchildren, who witnessed a tradition that is less common in their day-to-day lives but remains an anchor of cultural heritage. This celebration, therefore, not only honoured Ravi's age but also connected the younger generation to the values of reverence and family unity.

**Example 2: *Antim Samskara* - A Hindu Funeral and Mourning in Modern Context**

When Janaki, an 82-year-old grandmother from a Kannada family in Bengaluru, passed away, her family gathered to perform her last rites in accordance with Hindu traditions. In Hindu customs, funeral rites are seen as crucial for ensuring the soul's peaceful transition and release from worldly attachments. Janaki's son, Krishna, who lives in the United States, immediately flew to Bengaluru to fulfil his duties as the eldest son, which traditionally include lighting the funeral pyre and performing *Antim Samskara* (the final rites).

The family arranged a small gathering at Janaki's favourite temple, where her close relatives recited sacred verses and offered prayers. Following her cremation, Krishna and his siblings observed a 13-

day mourning period, during which they performed *Pinda Pradanam*, the offering of rice balls for the peace of her soul. Although Krishna needed to return to the United States, he performed a follow-up *Shraadha* ceremony a year later, through which he paid respect to his mother's spirit with the help of a priest who guided him virtually.

This experience was emotionally grounding for Krishna's children, who had grown up abroad and were less exposed to traditional customs. By participating in their grandmother's rituals, they gained an understanding of their cultural roots and were able to connect more deeply with the beliefs and values of their heritage. The blend of virtual and traditional elements demonstrated how rituals adapt to modern circumstances while still providing a meaningful way to process loss and honour one's ancestors.

# Part 4
# Financial and Legal Aspects

# Financial Planning for the Elderly in South Indian Context

As people grow older, financial planning becomes crucial for maintaining a stable and comfortable life in retirement. In India, this process holds unique cultural, social, and economic dimensions influenced by traditional family structures, spiritual values, and evolving lifestyle expectations. This section discusses essential aspects of financial planning for the elderly in the South Indian context, addressing the challenges, strategies, and tools available to support economic security and independence for the elderly.

**The Cultural Context of Financial Planning in South India**

In South India, family values traditionally play a significant role in an individual's retirement planning. Parents often expect to be supported by their children in old age, reflecting the cultural norm of intergenerational support. However, modern trends, such as nuclear family setups, migration, and increased life expectancy, have altered these expectations, necessitating personal financial planning to ensure self-sufficiency in later years.

The concept of financial independence during retirement is becoming increasingly prevalent. Elderly now strive to manage their finances autonomously, reducing dependency on children and ensuring that their personal needs are met without imposing financial pressure on the next generation.

**Key Components of Financial Planning for the Elderly**

Effective financial planning for the elderly involves a mix of investment strategies, risk management, tax planning, estate planning, and medical provisions. Each component must be tailored to meet the unique requirements of the elderly, who often prioritize safety, liquidity, and stability over high-risk, high-reward investment opportunities.

**a) Income Sources in Retirement**

Traditional income sources for the elderly include pension schemes, provident funds, annuities, rental income, and interest from fixed deposits or savings. Recent government-backed savings schemes offer additional options tailored to senior citizens, such as the Senior Citizens Savings Scheme (SCSS) and the Pradhan Mantri Vaya Vandana Yojana (PMVVY). For many, property rental income remains a dependable source of post-retirement earnings, especially among those who invested in real estate during their working years. The real estate market has shown steady appreciation, making it a favoured asset class for long-term investment. However, elderly individuals may need assistance with property management, rental agreements, and tenant relations, which family members or professionals often provide.

## b) Investment Strategies for Stability and Growth

While conservative investment options dominate the portfolios of elderly individuals, many are also looking to diversify for moderate growth. Popular investment choices include:

- **Fixed Deposits (FDs)**: Traditionally popular, FDs offer guaranteed returns and are ideal for individuals prioritizing financial security.
- **Public Provident Fund (PPF)**: Although PPFs have a 15-year lock-in period, they are considered stable, tax-free investment avenues that can provide periodic financial liquidity for the elderly through partial withdrawals after five years.
- **Mutual Funds**: Systematic Withdrawal Plans (SWPs) in mutual funds offer a structured method to generate periodic income, although these involve market risks. Debt funds and balanced funds are preferred for moderate risk and steady returns.
- **Real Estate Investment Trusts (REITs)**: For those hesitant to manage physical properties, REITs offer an indirect method of investing in real estate with lesser management obligations and steady returns through dividends.
- **Gold and Precious Metals**: Gold has traditional and sentimental value in Indian households. Gold Exchange Traded Funds (ETFs) and sovereign gold bonds offer ways to invest in gold without the need for physical safekeeping.

## c) Health and Medical Expense Planning

Healthcare costs are among the most significant financial burdens for elderly individuals, particularly in a country with limited public health coverage. South India has seen a rise in private healthcare facilities, and medical inflation often outpaces general inflation.

Investing in a comprehensive health insurance policy is paramount for managing these costs. For seniors without employer-provided coverage, policies like the Senior Citizen Health Insurance Scheme or private senior-specific plans offer coverage tailored to age-related health issues. The policy chosen must cover critical illnesses, outpatient care, and routine checkups.

Medical emergencies can cause severe financial strain, so a dedicated emergency fund, in addition to insurance, is advisable. Elderly individuals are encouraged to keep liquid assets equivalent to at least six months of expenses to manage unforeseen health-related costs.

**Challenges and Barriers in Financial Planning**

Financial planning for the elderly faces several challenges:
- **Lack of Financial Literacy**: Elderly individuals, especially those from rural areas, may lack the financial literacy required to understand complex financial products and manage investments.
- **Dependency on Family Members**: Many elderly individuals rely on family members for financial decisions. However, this dependency can be risky if family members do not prioritize their best interests.
- **Limited Access to Financial Services**: The elderly may have limited access to digital banking and other online financial services due to a lack of digital literacy, creating reliance on

physical bank branches, which are increasingly scarce in rural areas.
- **Inflation and Market Volatility**: Rising costs of living and market fluctuations can erode savings, making it critical to incorporate inflation-adjusted income sources in retirement plans.
- **Health-related Financial Strain**: Chronic health issues can consume a substantial portion of retirement funds, affecting other aspects of financial planning.

**Strategies for Financial Security and Independence**

Achieving financial security requires a mix of careful planning, risk mitigation, and regular review of financial goals. Here are some strategies to ensure independence and security for elderly individuals:

**a) Budgeting and Expense Management**

Maintaining a budget helps track monthly expenses and ensure that essential needs are met. Elderly individuals should focus on fixed and discretionary spending, prioritizing healthcare, household expenses, and other essentials. Budgeting also involves planning for festivals, family events, and charitable donations, all of which are culturally significant in South India.

**b) Estate and Succession Planning**

Estate planning ensures that assets are smoothly transferred to beneficiaries without legal disputes or family conflicts. This includes creating wills, power of attorney, and assigning a trustworthy executor. In India, where joint family ownership of assets is common, estate planning can help avoid misunderstandings and protect the interests of spouses or children.

**c) Tax Planning and Compliance**

Retirees in India are eligible for certain tax benefits. Seniors above 60 and super seniors above 80 receive higher tax exemption limits, making tax planning an essential part of financial management. Investments in tax-saving instruments, such as the SCSS and PPF, can help minimize tax liabilities, especially for elderly individuals with taxable incomes.

Income from fixed deposits, rental properties, and other investments should be managed to avoid excess tax burdens. Elderly individuals should also be aware of any exemptions or deductions available for medical expenses, as these can reduce taxable income significantly.

**d) Financial Protection from Fraud and Mismanagement**

The elderly are vulnerable to fraud due to limited familiarity with modern financial instruments or technology. Common fraud schemes include phishing, investment scams, and unauthorized withdrawals. Steps to mitigate these risks include:

- **Seeking Family or Professional Advice**: Consulting with trusted family members or a professional financial advisor ensures decisions are aligned with their best interests.
- **Using Digital Banking Safely**: Elderly individuals should be educated on digital banking security, avoiding unfamiliar calls or messages requesting sensitive information.

- **Limiting Dependence on Cash**: Elderly individuals often prefer cash transactions; however, maintaining limited cash holdings and instead using secure, trackable payments is safer.

**Government and Community Support for Financial Security**

The government of India has introduced several schemes to support the financial well-being of elderly citizens, which are especially beneficial to elderly in India. Some notable schemes include:

- **Senior Citizens Savings Scheme (SCSS)**: A safe investment option with regular income, SCSS is popular for those aged 60 and above, offering higher interest rates and regular income payouts.

- **Pradhan Mantri Vaya Vandana Yojana (PMVVY)**: This scheme offers a fixed monthly pension for 10 years, safeguarding against market volatility and ensuring steady income.

- **Atal Pension Yojana (APY)**: Available to all citizens, including seniors, this government-backed pension scheme ensures a lifetime income, with benefits continuing to the spouse after the subscriber's demise.

**Community Support Programs**

Several NGOs and community organizations provide financial counselling, health services, and support for elderly individuals. These programs aim to raise awareness about financial rights, assist in accessing government benefits, and offer counselling for financial literacy, health, and legal issues.

**The Role of Family in Elderly Financial Security**

Indian families traditionally assume responsibility for elderly members, with children supporting their parents' financial and emotional needs. As a result, financial planning often involves family discussions on shared responsibilities, inheritance, and caregiving expectations. Families can support elderly relatives by providing housing, contributing to health expenses, or assisting with financial management tasks.

**Encouraging Financial Autonomy**

At the same time, promoting financial autonomy is essential for the dignity and independence of elderly individuals. By encouraging older family members to maintain a separate account, manage their expenses, and make financial decisions, families can foster self-confidence and help them maintain control over their resources.

Financial planning for the elderly is essential to ensure a secure, dignified, and independent lifestyle in retirement. With rising life expectancy, increased health expenses, and shifting family structures, elderly must adopt comprehensive financial strategies. By focusing on stable investments, budgeting, tax planning, and health provisions, they can navigate the challenges of old age with confidence and ease.

Government support schemes, family involvement, and community resources all contribute to establishing a safety net for seniors, reflecting the collective responsibility the society places on caring for the elderly. Ultimately, the goal of financial planning is not only to ensure material well-being but also to empower seniors to lead fulfilling life.

**Example 1: Managing Retirement Savings and Healthcare Costs**

**Profile: Mrs. Anjali, 65 years old, from Chennai**

Mrs. Anjali is a retired school teacher living in Chennai. She receives a monthly pension of ₹30,000 and has accumulated savings of ₹15 lakhs in fixed deposits (FDs) and a Public Provident Fund (PPF). Additionally, she owns a small apartment in a well-developed neighbourhood, which she rents out for ₹12,000 per month.

**Financial Planning Steps**:

1. **Income Sources**:
   o Pension: ₹30,000/month
   o Rental Income: ₹12,000/month
   o Total Monthly Income: ₹42,000

2. **Monthly Expenses**:
   o Housing and Utilities: ₹10,000
   o Groceries and Daily Needs: ₹8,000
   o Healthcare and Medications: ₹5,000
   o Discretionary Expenses (entertainment, travel): ₹5,000
   o Total Monthly Expenses: ₹28,000

3. **Healthcare Planning**:
   o Understanding that healthcare costs can rise unexpectedly, Mrs. Anjali purchases a health insurance policy that covers hospitalization and outpatient expenses, ensuring that her total coverage is ₹5 lakhs.
   o She sets aside ₹1 lakh from her savings as an emergency fund for medical needs.

4. **Investment Strategy**:
   o To ensure steady growth of her funds, Mrs. Anjali invests ₹5 lakhs from her FD in a conservative balanced mutual fund, aiming for moderate returns with relatively low risk.
   o The remaining ₹10 lakhs stays in FDs, providing her with a guaranteed interest income.

5. **Long-term Financial Goals**:
o   Mrs. Anjali wishes to travel to religious and cultural sites in South India. She allocates ₹20,000 each year from her discretionary fund for this purpose.

**Outcome**: Mrs. Anjali's careful financial planning allows her to live comfortably within her means, ensuring that she can cover her essential expenses and healthcare costs while enjoying a fulfilling retirement life without depending on her children.

**Example 2: Intergenerational Financial Planning**

**Profile: Mr. Raghav, 72 years old, from Coimbatore**

Mr. Raghav is a retired bank manager who lives with his wife in Coimbatore. They have three children, all of whom are working professionals. He has a total of ₹25 lakhs in various investments, including FDs, a few shares, and a family-owned business.

**Financial Planning Steps**:

1. **Current Financial Assets**:
o   Fixed Deposits: ₹10 lakhs
o   Equity Shares: ₹5 lakhs
o   Family Business Value: ₹10 lakhs (which provides additional income)

2. **Monthly Income**:
   o Dividends from Shares and Business Income: ₹25,000/month
   o Interest from FDs: ₹7,000/month
   o Total Monthly Income: ₹32,000

3. **Family Discussions**:
   o Mr. Raghav holds family meetings to discuss financial planning, where he emphasizes the importance of investing wisely and planning for the future.
   o He shares his intent to transfer the family business to his children, highlighting that they should manage it while ensuring they provide him and his wife with regular financial support.

4. **Healthcare and Insurance**:
   o To mitigate health-related costs, Mr. Raghav purchases a comprehensive health insurance policy covering both him and his wife. They allocate ₹50,000 annually for premiums.
   o He sets aside an additional ₹2 lakhs in a savings account for future healthcare expenses.

5. **Estate Planning**:
   o Mr. Raghav drafts a will that clearly outlines the distribution of his assets, ensuring his children are well-informed about their inheritances and minimizing potential family disputes.
   o He establishes a power of attorney for financial and medical decisions, ensuring his wife's needs are prioritized.

**Outcome**: By engaging in open discussions and planning with his family, Mr. Raghav ensures financial stability for himself and his wife while also preparing for the seamless transition of the family business. This proactive approach secures his family's future and fosters a supportive environment for his children's involvement in managing family finances.

# Elderly and Property Rights in South Indian Families

In South Indian families, property ownership and inheritance are intricately linked with traditions, legal rights, and social responsibilities. The elderly hold a central place in these dynamics, often owning significant family property or serving as custodians of ancestral wealth. However, as they age, issues around property rights become more complex, intersecting with family relationships, societal norms, and legal frameworks. This write-up explores these dimensions in-depth, focusing on the legal rights of the elderly regarding property, common challenges they face, and cultural aspects that influence the distribution and transfer of property within families.

**Legal Framework of Property Rights for the Elderly**

The Indian legal system provides various provisions and laws to safeguard property rights for the elderly, particularly in the realm of inheritance, self-acquired property, and protection against property fraud and coercion.

- **Hindu Succession Act, 1956 (Amended 2005)**: For elderly Hindus in India, the Hindu Succession Act governs inheritance laws. The 2005 amendment recognized the equal rights of daughters in ancestral property, changing family dynamics and inheritance expectations. Elderly parents now often face the task of managing expectations from both sons and daughters, altering traditional patrilineal inheritance patterns.

- **Muslim Personal Law**: In India, elderly Muslims are subject to inheritance laws under Shariah. Unlike Hindu law, Muslim law prescribes fixed shares for heirs, ensuring a specific portion of inheritance for children and other relatives. This leaves less room for flexibility but offers clarity in property distribution for elderly Muslims.
- **Christian and Parsi Laws**: Christians and Parsis in India follow the Indian Succession Act, 1925, for property distribution, allowing elderly individuals to draft wills with fewer restrictions. This autonomy enables elderly Christians and Parsis to decide property distribution based on personal preference, sometimes generating familial conflict if the inheritance does not align with family expectations.
- **Maintenance and Welfare of Parents and Senior Citizens Act, 2007**: This act mandates that children and relatives are legally responsible for the maintenance of elderly parents. It also enables the elderly to reclaim their property if they have transferred it to a family member under the expectation of care that is later withdrawn or abused. This law has particular relevance, where cases of elderly individuals facing neglect from family members post-property transfer are rising.

**Common Issues Faced by the Elderly Regarding Property Rights**

Despite legal safeguards, the elderly in face unique challenges around property rights. These issues are often compounded by traditional expectations, family pressure, and in some cases, exploitation by younger family members.

- **Property Transfer Under Duress**: Due to cultural expectations of familial respect and obedience, elderly individuals may feel compelled to transfer property to children prematurely, often under pressure or persuasion. Sons or primary heirs might pressurize parents, citing the need for financial resources, business expansion, or dowries, leaving the elderly vulnerable to exploitation.
- **Lack of Awareness and Access to Legal Resources**: In India, a significant portion of the elderly, particularly in rural areas, remains unaware of their legal rights concerning property. A lack of awareness can lead to signing property documents without understanding the implications or falling prey to fraudulent practices by family members or external parties.
- **Conflicts with Sons, Daughters, and Extended Family**: With the modernization of inheritance laws and rising aspirations of family members, the elderly often face conflicts regarding property distribution. While daughters now have legal rights to ancestral property, traditional views still favour sons, leading to conflicts among siblings. Elderly parents may find themselves caught in family disputes, creating emotional and psychological stress.
- **Disinheritance and the Role of Wills**: The concept of drafting a will has gained traction, especially among elderly Christians and urban Hindus. However, the elderly might be influenced by certain family members when drafting wills, leading to partial or complete disinheritance of some heirs. Such actions often lead to disputes, with some family members challenging the will's authenticity.

- **Property Grabbing and Misuse of Trust**: Off late, India has witnessed cases where elderly individuals transfer property to family members in trust, only to find themselves neglected or even evicted. Instances of sons or daughters misusing elderly parents' goodwill to take control of property are not uncommon, highlighting the need for awareness and legal recourse for the elderly.

## Cultural Dimensions Influencing Elderly Property Rights

Cultural norms deeply influence property dynamics in families. While laws provide a framework, cultural practices often determine the practical application of these rights.

- **Patrilineal Inheritance and Family Obligations**: Traditionally, property has been transferred through the male lineage, with the eldest son or sons inheriting ancestral property. This has fostered expectations of male heirs' responsibility towards elderly parents, a belief that remains strong, especially in rural areas. Even with equal rights for daughters, elderly parents may still prioritize sons for property inheritance, viewing them as primary caretakers in old age.
- **Marriage and Dowry Practices**: Although legally discouraged, dowry practices remain prevalent, particularly in rural families. Many elderly parents feel obligated to provide significant property or financial assets as dowry for their daughters, affecting their own financial security. This transfer of property can also strain relationships with sons, who may feel their inheritance has been compromised.

- **Role of Religion and Faith**: In South Indian families, religious values often influence how property is handled. Hindu families, for instance, may follow certain rituals or consult astrologers when deciding on property division. Similarly, elderly Muslims may seek religious guidance regarding their property, adhering to Shariah principles even if family members prefer an alternative division.
- **Emotional Attachment to Ancestral Property**: For many elderly individuals, ancestral property holds deep emotional significance. Selling or dividing ancestral land or homes can lead to guilt or a sense of betrayal towards one's heritage. This attachment sometimes results in the elderly resisting division or sale, even when pressured by family members. It can also prompt the elderly to stipulate conditions in their wills, hoping to maintain the integrity of ancestral assets.

**Legal Safeguards and Solutions for the Elderly in Property Matters**

To address challenges faced by the elderly regarding property rights, there are several legal and practical measures that can be pursued.
- **Executing a Clear and Detailed Will**: A well-drafted will provides clarity and reduces the likelihood of disputes after the elderly person's passing. Legal aid centres and NGOs are now offering services to help the elderly draft wills with clear terms, reducing ambiguity in property distribution.
- **Utilizing the Maintenance and Welfare of Parents and Senior Citizens Act**: Under this act, elderly individuals can demand maintenance from children and, if necessary, reclaim property transferred under conditions of care. This act has proven to be

a valuable tool, enabling elderly individuals to safeguard their property from neglectful or exploitative relatives.
- **Setting Up Trusts and Legal Arrangements**: Some elderly establish trusts to secure their property. Trusts allow them to specify conditions under which property can be used, often preventing family members from unilaterally selling or misusing assets. Trusts are particularly beneficial for elderly individuals with substantial property who wish to retain control over its use.
- **Awareness and Legal Education**: Increased awareness of property rights among the elderly is essential. NGOs and legal advocacy groups play a role in educating elderly individuals about their rights, the process of transferring property, and protections against fraud. Many legal aid organizations also conduct seminars and workshops to inform the elderly of their options and avenues for assistance.
- **Counselling and Mediation Services**: Family conflicts over property can be emotionally taxing for the elderly. In many places, availability of mediation services through courts or community centres has provided some relief. These services offer a neutral space for elderly individuals to resolve property disputes amicably, reducing emotional strain and avoiding lengthy legal battles.

### Case Studies and Real-Life Examples

To further understand property rights issues faced by the elderly, let's look at some common scenarios.
- **Case of Premature Property Transfer**: In Chennai, an elderly widow transferred her property to her son, believing he would

care for her. However, after gaining ownership, he neglected her. With the help of local authorities and under the Maintenance and Welfare of Parents and Senior Citizens Act, she successfully reclaimed her property.

- **Dispute over Ancestral Property**: In a rural village in Karnataka, an elderly father faced resistance from his sons when attempting to divide ancestral land among all his children, including daughters. Despite legal backing, the sons argued that daughters should not receive land. After mediation and legal intervention, the father executed a will, ensuring equitable distribution among all children.
- **Trust Setup for Future Security**: An elderly couple in Hyderabad established a trust, specifying that their property could not be sold but would generate rental income for their grandchildren's education. This decision helped avoid potential disputes among children while preserving family property for future generations.

## Ensuring Dignity and Security for the Elderly in Property Matters

The issue of property rights for the elderly reflects the broader social and legal challenges they face. Balancing respect for cultural practices with legal protections is crucial to ensuring that the elderly can retain control over their assets while preserving family harmony. Legal frameworks offer valuable tools, but they must be supported by family awareness and sensitivity towards the elderly's rights. A collective effort, involving legal entities, family members, and society at large, can empower the elderly to navigate property

**Example 1: Conflict Over Ancestral Property**

**Background**: Rajan, a 78-year-old man from a traditional family in Tamil Nadu, is the custodian of his ancestral property—a large plot of agricultural land and a family home. Following the death of his wife, Rajan decides to divide his assets equally among his three children: two sons and a daughter. His daughter, Priya, lives in the same town and has a close bond with him, while both sons have moved to the city and have established their careers.

**Conflict**: When Rajan announces his decision to divide the property equally, his sons object. Citing traditional norms, they argue that the land should be divided only between them, claiming Priya is "married off" and her husband is expected to support her. The sons also pressurize Rajan by arguing that only male heirs are traditionally expected to inherit the property, questioning why their sister should have a share. They suggest that if Rajan insists on including Priya, they may have to cut ties with her.

**Emotional and Cultural Tensions**: Rajan faces intense emotional stress. He is torn between respecting his daughter's right to inherit and the backlash from his sons. Additionally, his community's perception that daughters should not inherit property adds pressure. Rajan fears that if he does not allocate property to Priya, she may struggle financially, especially if her husband's business falters. Yet, he also feels guilty for straying from tradition, fearing community disapproval.

**Resolution**: Rajan decides to seek legal counsel. With the lawyer's assistance, he drafts a will specifying an equal share of property for all his children, asserting his decision to prioritize fairness over tradition. Additionally, he includes a clause in his will mandating that none of his children can sell the land without mutual consent, preserving the integrity of the ancestral property. Though his sons are initially unhappy, Rajan's will offers clarity and ensures a balanced approach. Priya feels validated and reassured, knowing her father has acknowledged her rightful place in the family inheritance.

**Takeaway**: This example reflects the clash between tradition and legal rights families. Elderly individuals like Rajan face significant social and familial pressure, but legal frameworks such as the Hindu Succession Act empower them to make decisions based on fairness, promoting gender equality within family inheritance.

**Example 2: Coercion and Property Transfer Under Duress**

**Background**: Saraswati, a 75-year-old widow from Kerala, owns a modest house in her hometown and a small piece of agricultural land left by her late husband. Her only son, Ramesh, lives with her, along with his wife and two children. Ramesh has been pressuring his mother to transfer the property into his name, claiming that it would "simplify" future inheritance issues. Saraswati is hesitant, as she wants to retain control over her assets for her own security.

**Conflict**: Over time, Ramesh's insistence becomes more aggressive. He threatens to move out and stop supporting her if she refuses to transfer the property. Fearful of abandonment, Saraswati reluctantly signs over her property, hoping her son will fulfil his promise to care for her. However, once Ramesh gains ownership, his behaviour changes. He becomes indifferent and leaves her care primarily to his wife, who is also unenthusiastic about the responsibility. Saraswati finds herself feeling neglected, isolated, and regretful about the decision.

**Legal Intervention**: Saraswati shares her troubles with a friend, who informs her of the Maintenance and Welfare of Parents and Senior Citizens Act, 2007. With her friend's encouragement, she approaches a local legal aid office, which guides her through the process of filing a case. Under the Act, she seeks to reclaim her property, arguing that the transfer was based on the promise of care that was not upheld.

**Outcome**: After a court hearing, Saraswati successfully reclaims her property. Ramesh is ordered to pay a monthly maintenance amount, ensuring her financial independence. The case gains local attention, serving as a reminder within the community of the legal rights available to elderly parents in similar situations. Saraswati now feels empowered, with her property returned and her financial security reinforced.

**Takeaway**: This example highlights how elderly individuals may experience coercion from family members regarding property transfer. The Maintenance and Welfare of Parents and Senior Citizens Act protects elderly individuals from such exploitation, providing a legal recourse that allows them to maintain control over their assets and secure their well-being.

# Government Policies and Schemes for the Elderly

As India's population ages, the needs of its elderly have become increasingly significant. A substantial portion of the elderly population resides where traditional family structures are evolving under the influence of urbanization and migration. This demographic shift has led to a growing demand for policies and schemes tailored to support the elderly's well-being, independence, and dignity. In response, the Indian government has implemented several policies to address financial, healthcare, and social security needs for senior citizens. This chapter outlines key policies and schemes, assesses their efficacy, and examines their impact on urban families.

**The National Policy on Older Persons (1999)**

The National Policy on Older Persons (NPOP) was one of the earliest policy frameworks aimed at ensuring senior citizens' dignity, financial security, and healthcare access. The policy's objectives include providing social support, financial assistance, and access to healthcare and housing. However, the policy is more than two decades old, and demographic, economic, and social changes necessitate an update.

For elderly, this policy initially provided support mechanisms, but its relevance has waned, given the shifting family dynamics in urban areas. The policy's objectives remain crucial; however, implementation gaps persist, especially in reaching elderly individuals from economically weaker backgrounds who are no longer part of traditional family setups.

## The Maintenance and Welfare of Parents and Senior Citizens Act (2007)

The Maintenance and Welfare of Parents and Senior Citizens Act mandates that adult children provide financial support to their elderly parents. If they fail to do so, parents have the legal right to claim maintenance. The act empowers senior citizens, especially those from low-income families, to seek support from their families and offers protection against neglect and abandonment.

While culturally rooted in South India, where familial respect and caregiving are valued, this policy has become increasingly relevant in urban areas. South Indian cities are experiencing high rates of migration, often leaving elderly parents alone or financially insecure. The act provides a legal recourse but relies on a legal framework that is often inaccessible to those who may not be familiar with the procedures involved. Awareness campaigns on this act, particularly in vernacular languages, are essential in South Indian states to ensure more people benefit from this protection.

### Indira Gandhi National Old Age Pension Scheme (IGNOAPS)

The Indira Gandhi National Old Age Pension Scheme (IGNOAPS) provides a minimum monthly pension to senior citizens who fall below the poverty line. Managed under the National Social

Assistance Programme (NSAP), this scheme aims to alleviate poverty among senior citizens by offering a modest monthly pension. However, the scheme faces limitations: it offers a small monthly amount that often proves insufficient to meet basic needs, and the eligibility criteria can be restrictive.

In the urban context, elderly people from lower-income backgrounds greatly benefit from such schemes, yet they often face challenges in accessing them due to bureaucratic procedures and lack of awareness. Additionally, the varying socio-economic levels across states necessitate a more nuanced approach, potentially with increased pension amounts or a reduction in eligibility restrictions for the economically vulnerable.

**Integrated Programme for Senior Citizens (IPSrC)**

The Integrated Programme for Senior Citizens (IPSrC) is a scheme that provides financial assistance to NGOs and other agencies to run day-care centres, old-age homes, and mobile healthcare units for the elderly. This program plays a crucial role in supporting elderly individuals who are either single or do not have family support.

The success of this scheme in the South Indian states varies. Kerala, for example, has seen relatively successful implementation due to its high literacy rate and strong presence of NGOs. However, in other states, especially in urban areas, the scheme's impact has been limited. To bridge this gap, there is a need for public-private partnerships that could extend its reach. Collaborations with community centres in urban areas could increase the accessibility of these services, helping to integrate elder care into the daily lives of seniors.

**Atal Vayo Abhyuday Yojana (AVAY)**

The Atal Vayo Abhyuday Yojana, launched in 2020, aims to promote a dignified life for senior citizens through an improved, accessible healthcare system. This scheme is part of a broader governmental commitment to ensure healthcare and housing support, including efforts to support longevity, independence, and quality of life. Through AVAY, the government offers support to states and NGOs, creating an infrastructure conducive to elderly welfare and care.

In South India, where healthcare systems are relatively better developed in states like Tamil Nadu and Kerala, AVAY could have a significant impact if its services are effectively coordinated with state healthcare policies. However, the rural-urban divide still poses a challenge. In the urban centres, senior citizens might have access to better facilities, but the program could also benefit rural elders by increasing healthcare outreach efforts and introducing telemedicine options.

**Healthcare Schemes for Senior Citizens**

The healthcare needs of senior citizens are prioritized in several government health schemes. For instance, the **Ayushman Bharat Pradhan Mantri Jan Arogya Yojana** (AB-PMJAY) provides health insurance coverage to economically weaker sections, including senior citizens. This scheme offers access to secondary and tertiary healthcare, covering major treatments that could financially drain families. For senior citizens, especially those suffering from chronic illnesses, this scheme provides significant relief.

In states like Karnataka and Tamil Nadu have aligned their healthcare systems with AB-PMJAY, and Kerala has its state-specific **Karunya Arogya Suraksha Padhathi** (KASP). These schemes relieve the financial strain on families and give elderly patients access to quality healthcare. Yet, the effectiveness of these schemes in urban settings depends on healthcare infrastructure and the availability of healthcare providers who understand geriatric needs.

Another crucial healthcare initiative is the **National Programme for Health Care of the Elderly (NPHCE)**, which provides geriatric healthcare services through the public health system. It includes geriatric wards in district hospitals and health services in rural primary health centres (PHCs). Although NPHCE is a step forward, the program needs further expansion in urban areas, where specialized geriatric facilities in hospitals are still limited.

**Reverse Mortgage Scheme**

The Reverse Mortgage Scheme, introduced by the National Housing Bank, allows elderly individuals to mortgage their homes to banks in exchange for regular income. This scheme targets those who are "asset-rich but cash-poor," providing financial security for seniors who may not have other income sources.

In cities and towns, where property values are relatively high, this scheme could serve as a viable option for elderly homeowners. However, uptake has been limited due to cultural barriers, as property is often considered an inheritance for the next generation. Awareness campaigns and counselling services are essential to educate seniors and families about how the scheme works and its benefits for elderly independence.

**Tax Benefits for Senior Citizens**

The Indian government offers several tax benefits to senior citizens, including higher income tax exemption limits and deductions on health insurance premiums. For instance, the exemption limit for individuals aged 60 and above is higher than that for younger taxpayers, and those over 80 have an even higher exemption threshold. Additionally, Section 80D allows deductions for health insurance premiums, which is especially useful as healthcare costs tend to rise with age.

For middle-income urban families, these tax exemptions ease the financial burden, especially given the rising costs of private healthcare. However, awareness of these benefits is not widespread, and many elderly citizens may not fully understand how to utilize them effectively. Workshops and informational campaigns focused on tax planning for senior citizens could enhance the benefits of these provisions.

**Pradhan Mantri Vaya Vandana Yojana (PMVVY)**

The Pradhan Mantri Vaya Vandana Yojana (PMVVY) is a pension scheme managed by the Life Insurance Corporation of India (LIC). It offers a guaranteed return rate for a period of 10 years, with monthly, quarterly, or annual payouts. This scheme is especially useful for senior citizens looking for a secure investment that provides regular income.

In several cities, where the cost of living can be higher, PMVVY is a valuable tool for financial stability among retired individuals. However, LIC's reach and awareness campaigns should be strengthened to educate urban elders on this scheme's long-term benefits. As financial literacy among the elderly may vary, especially in smaller towns, easy-to-understand resources would be helpful.

**Challenges and Recommendations**

Although government schemes exist to support the elderly, there are several challenges to their effective implementation. The key issues include lack of awareness, bureaucratic barriers, and inadequate monitoring. Specific steps can be taken to improve these schemes' outreach and efficiency:

1. **Improving Awareness**: Many elderly citizens, particularly in semi urban areas, remain unaware of their rights and the support available to them. This is particularly relevant in South India, where linguistic and cultural diversity calls for localized, language-specific awareness campaigns.
2. **Streamlining Access**: Simplifying application procedures for senior citizen benefits and integrating digital solutions, with assistance available in local languages, can make these schemes more accessible.
3. **Geriatric Care Training for Healthcare Providers**: Implementing geriatric care training programs in urban

hospitals can greatly enhance healthcare services for the elderly.
4. **Expanding Public-Private Partnerships**: Collaborating with NGOs, private healthcare providers, and senior citizen organizations could improve the reach and efficacy of government schemes.
5. **Strengthening Legal Awareness**: Programs promoting the Maintenance and Welfare of Parents and Senior Citizens Act should be organized to educate families on legal obligations and encourage family support systems.

**Example 1:** *Venkatesh and the Maintenance and Welfare of Parents and Senior Citizens Act (2007)*

Venkatesh, a retired schoolteacher in Bengaluru, had always envisioned a peaceful retirement surrounded by family. However, as his children moved abroad for better career opportunities, Venkatesh found himself living alone, managing his finances on a limited pension. Although he received some support from his children, it wasn't sufficient to cover medical expenses and rising living costs. His children visited infrequently and gradually reduced financial support, citing their own financial commitments. One day, Venkatesh attended a local senior citizens' meeting, where he learned about the **Maintenance and Welfare of Parents and Senior Citizens Act (2007)**. This act mandates that adult children must provide financial support to their parents if they are unable to sustain themselves. Venkatesh reached out to a local legal aid centre, which helped him send a legal notice to his children, requesting a fixed monthly amount for his expenses. After a few formalities and discussions, his children agreed to provide regular financial assistance. The act provided Venkatesh with the confidence and legal backing to seek support without straining familial ties.For seniors like Venkatesh, the act offers crucial protection, particularly in cities where elderly parents often feel hesitant to ask for support. This example illustrates how legal frameworks empower elderly individuals and preserve their dignity, even as family dynamics change in urban settings.

**Example 2:** *Lakshmi and the Ayushman Bharat Pradhan Mantri Jan Arogya Yojana (AB-PMJAY)*

Lakshmi, a 72-year-old widow from Chennai, was diagnosed with chronic kidney disease, requiring frequent dialysis and specialized care. Her limited savings and pension were quickly drained by the high cost of treatments, placing her in a difficult financial position. Her son supported her as much as he could, but with his own family to support, it was challenging. Lakshmi's neighbour informed her about the **Ayushman Bharat Pradhan Mantri Jan Arogya Yojana (AB-PMJAY)**, which provides financial assistance for healthcare treatments to economically weaker families, including seniors. After verifying her eligibility, she successfully enrolled in the scheme. This allowed her to access subsidized dialysis sessions at a private hospital nearby, significantly reducing her medical expenses. The scheme's support eased Lakshmi's financial burden and allowed her son to focus on his family's needs as well. This example highlights the transformative impact of healthcare schemes like AB-PMJAY, especially in urban settings where healthcare costs are high. It demonstrates how these policies can directly improve the quality of life for elderly citizens, alleviating both medical and financial stress.

# Legal Challenges: Elder Abuse, Rights, and Protection

As families and communities evolve, the elderly population faces unique legal challenges that often remain underexplored. In this chapter, we delve into the complexities of elder abuse, legal rights, and protection mechanisms within the Indian context. By examining the specific forms of elder abuse, the legal landscape for elderly rights, and the mechanisms for protection, this section aims to provide a comprehensive understanding of the legal concerns and available resources for elderly individuals.

**Understanding Elder Abuse**

Elder abuse refers to any form of mistreatment or exploitation that results in harm or distress to an elderly person. This abuse can be physical, emotional, financial, or even neglectful. Studies have shown that elder abuse in India, including in the southern states, is largely underreported, with many cases going unrecognized due to social stigma, cultural norms, and the lack of legal literacy among the elderly and their families.

**Forms of Elder Abuse**
1. **Physical Abuse**: This includes inflicting pain or injury through physical force. Incidents of physical abuse may not always be overtly violent; they can also be subtle forms of mistreatment like withholding food or medical care.

2. **Emotional/Psychological Abuse**: Psychological abuse, such as verbal insults, humiliation, or isolating the elder from social interactions, is among the most common forms of elder abuse. Emotional abuse often leaves no visible scars but deeply affects the mental health and well-being of the elderly.
3. **Financial Abuse**: This involves unauthorized access to the elder's finances, property, or assets. Financial abuse can take many forms, including misusing the elder's funds, manipulating wills or property deeds, and coercing the elder into transferring assets.
4. **Neglect**: Neglect, or the failure to provide necessary care, is often seen when family members or caregivers ignore the basic needs of the elderly. This can include failing to provide adequate food, shelter, or medical attention.
5. **Abandonment**: Abandonment occurs when an elder is deserted by their caregiver or family members, leaving them helpless. In India, with its strong cultural emphasis on familial support, abandonment often goes unnoticed until it reaches an extreme stage.

## Legal Frameworks for Elder Rights and Protection in India

In India, the legal frameworks addressing elder abuse and protection are relatively recent, largely influenced by the global focus on human rights and the growing recognition of elder care as a priority. Although these frameworks apply nationally, there are unique social and cultural implications for their implementation in states, such as Tamil Nadu, Karnataka, Kerala, Andhra Pradesh, and Telangana.

**The Maintenance and Welfare of Parents and Senior Citizens Act, 2007**

The Maintenance and Welfare of Parents and Senior Citizens Act, 2007, is a landmark legislation that underscores the obligation of children to provide financial support and basic necessities for their elderly parents. Here are the primary aspects of this law:

1. **Maintenance Claims**: This Act mandates children and legal heirs to provide maintenance for parents and senior citizens if they are unable to meet their financial needs. Elders can file a claim in the designated Maintenance Tribunal for a monthly allowance.
2. **Role of the Maintenance Tribunal**: The Maintenance Tribunal expedites cases and is mandated to pass an order within 90 days. In South India, states have established district-wise tribunals to ensure that elders have access to these forums, with hearings conducted in a supportive and accessible environment.
3. **Reverse Mortgage Provision**: This Act promotes reverse mortgage schemes, which allow elders to convert their homes into a source of income, providing financial security while continuing to live in their own homes.
4. **Protection Against Forced Dispossession**: The Act prevents children from forcibly evicting their parents from property that the elder owns or lives in. This provision holds significant relevance in households, where intergenerational living is common, and disputes over property can lead to elder homelessness.

## The Rights of Persons with Disabilities Act, 2016

The Rights of Persons with Disabilities Act, 2016, recognizes the rights of elderly individuals with disabilities. This Act mandates reasonable accommodations for elders with physical, sensory, or cognitive impairments and ensures that government and private establishments provide equal access to services, infrastructure, and opportunities.

## Criminal Laws Addressing Elder Abuse

In addition to specific acts, Indian criminal laws provide mechanisms to address elder abuse. Section 498A of the Indian Penal Code (IPC), which addresses cruelty by family members, is occasionally invoked in cases involving elder abuse. Further, Section 125 of the IPC provides elderly parents with a legal pathway to seek maintenance if their children fail to support them financially.

## The Domestic Violence Act, 2005

While often associated with spousal abuse, the Domestic Violence Act, 2005, also applies to elderly individuals living in a shared household. This Act allows elders to seek legal protection from family members or caregivers who subject them to abuse, providing both civil and criminal remedies. However, due to limited awareness, elders rarely utilize this Act.

## Challenges in Legal Recourse for Elder Abuse

Despite these legal frameworks, elderly individuals face significant challenges when seeking recourse.

### Social and Cultural Barriers

In Indian culture, strong emphasis is placed on familial ties and respect for elders. This cultural framework sometimes creates barriers for elders to report abuse due to the fear of stigmatizing the family or losing familial support. Furthermore, elderly individuals are often reluctant to engage in legal disputes with their children due to emotional attachment and social pressure.

### Lack of Awareness and Accessibility

Many elders, particularly those in rural areas, are unaware of their legal rights and available resources. This lack of awareness, coupled with limited access to legal aid, hinders elders from effectively seeking justice. In urban areas, although legal services may be more accessible, bureaucratic red tape and procedural delays deter many elderly individuals from initiating legal action.

### Financial Constraints

Legal proceedings in India can be costly, and many elders are unable to bear the financial burden. Although legal aid is available, the accessibility and quality of free legal services vary across regions. Elders from economically disadvantaged backgrounds are especially vulnerable to abuse and exploitation due to their limited financial resources.

**Judicial and Administrative Delays**

The Indian judicial system is often criticized for delays in case resolution, and elderly litigants suffer disproportionately from these delays. For the elderly population, time is of the essence, and prolonged litigation can result in significant mental and emotional distress.

**Protection Mechanisms and Support Services**

**Helplines and Reporting Mechanisms**

States such as Tamil Nadu, Karnataka and Kerala have made strides in establishing helplines and support services for the elderly. For instance, "Elder Helplines" provide immediate assistance to seniors, including counselling, legal aid, and police intervention in cases of abuse. The helpline numbers, accessible across districts, are often publicized through media, local governance bodies, and community centres.

**NGOs and Community-Based Organizations**

Numerous non-governmental organizations (NGOs) and community-based organizations offer support services for elders, including legal aid, financial support, and rehabilitation. Organizations like HelpAge India play a crucial role in supporting elder abuse victims, providing them with emergency services, legal counsel, and shelter.

**Senior Citizens Associations**

Senior citizens associations serve as a social and legal resource, particularly in urban parts of the country. These associations empower elders by providing a collective voice to advocate for their rights. They also organize legal awareness workshops, health camps, and community-building activities to combat isolation and vulnerability among the elderly.

**Police and Legal Aid Services**

Law enforcement agencies are gradually becoming more sensitive to elder abuse cases. Police departments now have dedicated officers trained to handle elder abuse cases with empathy and patience. Legal aid services are also expanding, with provisions for senior citizens to access free or subsidized legal services, especially for maintenance claims and property disputes.

**Recommendations for Strengthening Elder Rights and Protection**

1. **Enhanced Awareness Programs**: Government bodies, NGOs, and senior citizen associations should collaborate to conduct awareness programs focusing on elder rights and legal protections, particularly in rural and semi-urban settings. These programs should address the stigma surrounding elder abuse and encourage elders to report mistreatment.

2. **Expansion of Legal Aid Services**: Expanding legal aid services specific to elder abuse cases would help elderly individuals seek justice without financial burdens. These services should prioritize speedy case resolution, given the time-sensitive nature of elder issues.

3. **Sensitizing Law Enforcement**: Police and law enforcement personnel should be regularly trained in handling elder abuse cases. Sensitivity training can improve law enforcement's approach to elderly complainants, ensuring they feel respected and understood.

4. **Increased Use of Mediation and Counselling**: Many elder abuse cases can be resolved outside of the courtroom through mediation and family counselling. Mediation services, facilitated by legal experts and social workers, can help resolve conflicts in a manner that respects family bonds while ensuring elder protection.

5. **Stronger Implementation of Reverse Mortgage Schemes**: The governments in collaboration with financial institutions should promote reverse mortgage schemes as a viable option for financially vulnerable elders. Greater access to financial resources can reduce elders' dependence on their children and prevent financial exploitation.

6. **Community Vigilance Programs**: Establishing community-based vigilance programs can help prevent elder abuse at

the grassroots level. Community members can act as the first line of defence by observing and reporting signs of abuse, creating a protective environment for elders.

7. **Regular Review of Legal Frameworks**: Laws protecting elders should be reviewed periodically to address emerging issues, such as digital financial exploitation and online scams targeting seniors. Legal frameworks should evolve to encompass the changing socio-economic landscape.

The legal challenges surrounding elder abuse, rights, and protection reflect broader issues within Indian society, including the complexities of familial obligations, cultural norms, and the vulnerabilities of an aging population. Although India has implemented several laws to protect the elderly, these legal frameworks are only as effective as their implementation and the willingness of society to acknowledge and address elder abuse. By fostering awareness, accessibility, and a compassionate approach to elder rights, the country can create a society that respects and safeguards its elderly, honouring the wisdom and dignity they bring to the community.

---

**Case Study 1: Financial Exploitation and Emotional Abuse in Urban Bangalore**

**Background**: Mrs. Kamala Ramesh, a 75-year-old widow, lives in a prime area in Bangalore. She inherited her husband's property and had substantial savings from his pension. After her husband's death, Kamala's son, who lived with his family abroad, encouraged her to continue living independently with periodic visits from him. As her health began to decline, her son suggested that she give him the power of attorney to "manage her financial matters" more efficiently. Trusting her son, Kamala agreed.

**Incident**: Over time, Kamala noticed unusual changes in her finances. Large amounts of money were being transferred out of her accounts, and her monthly budget for necessities was gradually reduced. She also noticed that her son was becoming distant, with his calls and visits becoming rare. When she confronted him, he justified the withdrawals as "necessary investments" and dismissed her concerns, leaving her feeling emotionally distressed and isolated.

One day, she overheard from a neighbour that her son was trying to sell her property. Alarmed, Kamala approached her local senior citizens association, where she learned about her legal rights regarding financial abuse and property rights.

**Legal Action and Challenges**:

1. **Filing a Complaint**: With the help of the senior citizens association, Kamala filed a complaint under the Maintenance and Welfare of Parents and Senior Citizens Act, 2007, seeking revocation of the power of attorney and demanding her son provide regular maintenance. The association helped her reach out to the Bangalore District Maintenance Tribunal, which handles cases related to elderly maintenance and abuse.

2. **Revocation of Power of Attorney**: With legal assistance, Kamala was able to revoke the power of attorney she had granted to her son. She also filed a case for a monthly allowance to cover her living expenses, as she was financially dependent on her son after his mismanagement of her savings.

3. **Emotional Support and Counselling**: Recognizing Kamala's emotional trauma, the senior citizens association also facilitated counselling sessions for her, helping her cope with the psychological impact of her son's betrayal.

**Outcome and Learning**: The tribunal ruled in Kamala's favour, ordering her son to return the misappropriated funds and provide her with a monthly allowance. The tribunal also restricted her son from engaging in any future transactions involving her property. Kamala's story highlights the importance of educating elders about their financial and legal rights, as well as the support available through local senior organizations and the Maintenance Tribunal.

In metropolitan cities, where property values are high, cases like Kamala's are increasingly common. This case underscores the significance of having legal safeguards such as the Maintenance Act and local senior citizen associations to empower elders to reclaim their rights and protect their assets from exploitation by family members.

### Case Study 2: Physical and Emotional Neglect in Rural Tamil Nadu

**Background**: Mr. Natarajan, 80, lives in a small village in Tamil Nadu and is completely dependent on his son and daughter-in-law for daily care. His wife passed away several years ago, and since then, he has relied on his son for basic needs. Natarajan's health deteriorated due to arthritis, which limited his mobility, and he began suffering from age-related conditions, including memory issues.

**Incident**: Over time, Natarajan's son and daughter-in-law began neglecting his care. They provided minimal food, left him in unsanitary conditions, and ignored his medical needs. They often left him alone for extended periods, causing him emotional distress. The neglect worsened to the point that Natarajan developed infections due to unhygienic living conditions and lacked basic medications. Despite his suffering, he was afraid to seek help, fearing he would be abandoned by his only family.

Fortunately, a neighbour noticed Natarajan's condition and contacted a local NGO working in elder care. Representatives from the NGO visited Natarajan, documenting his condition and encouraging him to seek help.

**Legal Action and Challenges**:

1. **Initiating a Complaint under the Maintenance Act**: With the NGO's assistance, Natarajan filed a complaint with the Maintenance Tribunal, requesting maintenance from his son. Given Natarajan's frail health, the NGO also requested the court to consider his immediate care needs and arrange a temporary caregiver if necessary.
2. **Challenges in a Rural Setting**: The legal process was challenging, as rural elders like Natarajan often lack direct access to legal assistance. Language barriers and the local

perception of family loyalty also hindered Natarajan's initial willingness to proceed. However, the NGO's involvement ensured that Natarajan received legal representation and translation services.

3. **Involving Law Enforcement and Medical Assistance**: The NGO advocated for police intervention to investigate potential elder abuse and collaborated with local health authorities to provide Natarajan with immediate medical care. A medical report confirmed signs of severe neglect, strengthening his case in court.

**Outcome and Learning**: The tribunal mandated that Natarajan's son provide adequate food, shelter, and a monthly allowance to ensure his father's well-being. Additionally, the NGO arranged periodic welfare checks on Natarajan to prevent further neglect. His son faced a stern warning from the tribunal, highlighting the legal ramifications of continued neglect.

This case illustrates the unique barriers faced by elders in rural India, where access to legal resources is limited, and social stigma discourages elders from taking action against their family members. Organizations like NGOs play a vital role in bridging these gaps by offering support, legal aid, and coordination with health services. Furthermore, it underscores the critical need for increased legal awareness among rural elders to empower them to take action against neglect and abuse.

# Part 5

# Senior Living and Care Options

# Living Arrangements: At Home vs. Senior Living Communities

As India's population ages, the question of how best to accommodate the elderly—especially within families steeped in tradition and close-knit family values—gains significant importance. Traditionally, Indian society has revered the elderly, giving them places of respect and often expecting younger generations to care for them. However, with socio-economic transformations, urbanization, and shifting family dynamics, the choice between staying at home and moving to a senior living community has emerged as a critical one. This chapter explores the nuances of these options, particularly from a South Indian perspective, where family structures, cultural expectations, and financial constraints influence the living arrangements of the elderly.

**The Cultural Importance of Aging at Home in South India**

In South Indian culture, a profound value is placed on familial bonds, generational respect, and the concept of "living together." The idea of children taking care of their aging parents is deeply ingrained, rooted in both the Hindu dharma of *Pitru Rina* (a duty towards one's parents) and the cultural ethos of honouring and protecting elders. Traditionally, elderly parents live with their children and grandchildren, often in multi-generational households. This arrangement fosters social support, emotional security, and companionship, all within a familiar cultural setting. For many families, the presence of elders at home is also a spiritual blessing. The elderly are often seen as carriers of wisdom, familial traditions, and spiritual guidance. Consequently, living arrangements that move them away from the family unit can appear, to some, as neglectful or culturally insensitive. However, urbanization, nuclear families, and the professional demands of younger generations are challenging this traditional model.

**Factors Influencing Living Arrangements in South India**

The decision regarding living arrangements for elderly individuals is complex, impacted by several interwoven factors:

1. **Family Structure and Lifestyle:** With more nuclear families and children living overseas or in distant cities, caring for elders at home can become a logistical challenge.
2. **Health and Mobility:** Aging individuals with chronic health conditions or limited mobility often require specialized care that can be difficult to provide at home. Senior living communities often offer medical facilities and emergency care, addressing this concern.
3. **Financial Considerations:** The cost of eldercare is an important factor. Many families may struggle to provide in-home care, particularly if it requires employing full-time caregivers, installing accessibility modifications, or other financial investments.
4. **Elderly Preferences:** Some seniors may prefer staying within their familiar environments, while others may feel isolated and desire socialization opportunities offered by senior living communities.

5. **Cultural Sensitivity:** The decision is often weighed with cultural expectations, and for some families, moving an elder to a senior living facility may seem culturally inappropriate.
6. **Social Support:** Living arrangements that ensure regular social interaction, companionship, and participation in cultural activities contribute significantly to mental health and wellbeing.

**Living at Home: The Advantages and Challenges**

Living at home allows elders to remain within their own surroundings, where they feel comfortable and connected to their memories, belongings, and community. Many elders find solace in maintaining familiar routines, attending local temples, participating in neighbourhood events, and engaging in traditional rituals.

**Advantages of Living at Home**

1. **Familiarity and Comfort:** Familiar settings provide emotional comfort and security, helping elders maintain their independence and dignity.
2. **Family Interaction:** Being close to family members allows elders to be part of their children's and grandchildren's lives, maintaining the familial bonds that are central to the culture.
3. **Community Ties:** Elders living in their home environment can continue to interact with their local community and participate in cultural or religious gatherings.

4. **Cultural Continuity:** Living at home allows elderly individuals to observe traditional practices in a more authentic environment. From celebrating festivals to following daily spiritual practices, they retain the cultural ties integral to their identity.

**Challenges of Living at Home**

1. **Lack of Medical and Emergency Care:** Homes may lack the medical facilities required for elders who need regular monitoring or immediate medical assistance.
2. **Physical Barriers:** Many homes are not equipped to accommodate mobility-impaired seniors. Modifying homes to meet accessibility needs can be costly and challenging.
3. **Caregiver Strain:** Family members may struggle with the physical, emotional, and financial demands of caregiving. Additionally, balancing professional and caregiving responsibilities can lead to burnout.
4. **Social Isolation:** As peers and friends move away or pass on, some elders may feel increasingly isolated. Living at home might exacerbate loneliness if they have limited social interaction outside the family.

**Senior Living Communities: An Emerging Option**

Over the last decade, senior living communities have gained popularity, with many offering a blend of independent living, assisted care, and medical services. Designed to cater to the needs of the elderly, these communities balance the need for medical attention, social engagement, and cultural relevance. They have also diversified, with some focusing on specific cultural, linguistic, or religious groups, catering to the specific expectations of the elders.

**Advantages of Senior Living Communities**

1. **Health and Wellness Services:** Many senior living communities have in-house doctors, wellness programs, and emergency care facilities that provide round-the-clock assistance.
2. **Engagement and Socialization:** Senior communities organize social, cultural, and recreational activities tailored to the elderly. This fosters a sense of belonging and helps prevent loneliness.
3. **Safety and Security:** These communities are equipped with security measures and emergency protocols to ensure a safe living environment for seniors.
4. **Customized Care Options:** From independent living to assisted care, these communities offer a range of services, allowing seniors to receive support suited to their health and mobility levels.
5. **Freedom from Domestic Responsibilities:** In senior living communities, the elderly are relieved from household chores, allowing them to focus on hobbies, health, and relaxation.
6. **Cultural Adaptation:** Senior living communities that cater specifically to South Indian seniors often organize traditional events, religious celebrations, and festivals, helping maintain cultural continuity.

## Challenges of Senior Living Communities

1. **Cost and Affordability:** Many senior living facilities come with high costs, making them accessible primarily to upper-middle and affluent families. For some families, the cost of maintaining an elderly relative in a senior living facility can be prohibitive.
2. **Social Stigma:** Some traditional families still view senior living communities with scepticism, seeing them as an abandonment of duty. Convincing elders and extended family members of the advantages can be challenging due to cultural resistance.
3. **Adjustment Difficulties:** For elders who have lived in the same environment for decades, the transition to a community setting can be disorienting and emotionally taxing.
4. **Individual Preferences:** Some elderly individuals may feel constrained by the regimented lifestyle in senior living communities, missing the autonomy and unique comforts of their own homes.

## Comparative Analysis: At Home vs. Senior Living Communities

1. **Health Support:** Senior living communities offer dedicated medical support, reducing the stress on families to provide care. In contrast, in-home care may require hiring health professionals, which can be costly and may lack 24/7 availability.

2. **Social Interaction:** Senior living communities encourage social interaction with peers, reducing loneliness. However, living at home ensures daily interaction with family, fostering closer intergenerational bonds.
3. **Cultural Sensitivity:** Living at home allows for greater adherence to cultural practices, which is especially significant in South India. Some senior living communities, however, are beginning to incorporate cultural elements such as temple visits, festivals, and regional cuisines.
4. **Independence vs. Structure:** At home, elders retain more autonomy over daily routines, while senior living communities often have structured schedules. Some elders may prefer this structure, while others might find it restrictive.
5. **Economic Considerations:** Financially, maintaining an elder at home may be less costly than a high-end senior living facility, though this depends on the required level of care and location.

**Emerging Trends and Hybrid Models**

Recognizing the growing demand for varied eldercare solutions, hybrid models are emerging. For instance, assisted living facilities provide temporary care, allowing elders to return home after recovery or during family vacations. Some companies are also offering senior-specific home modification services, adapting homes to better suit elders' needs without requiring them to move out.

In addition, the growth of *home health care services* in Urban South India has offered a middle-ground option. These services provide caregivers, nurses, or even part-time companions to elderly people in their own homes, bridging the gap between full-time family caregiving and senior living communities. This enables seniors to continue living at home while receiving the necessary support, addressing some of the common challenges associated with aging in place.

The decision between living at home and moving to a senior living community is nuanced, influenced by factors like family structure, financial resources, health needs, and personal preferences. While living at home aligns with traditional values of familial closeness, senior living communities provide practical solutions for families struggling to balance modern demands with eldercare. Ultimately, the best choice is one that respects the elder's preferences, maintains their dignity, and ensures their health and happiness.

The eldercare landscape is likely to continue evolving as families find creative ways to honour traditions while adapting to new realities. This flexibility will be essential in creating solutions that respect cultural values while addressing practical concerns, ensuring that the elderly receive the care and respect they deserve as they age.

**Example 1: Living at Home with Family in Bangalore**

**Background** Seventy-five-year-old Mr. Narayan Iyer has lived in his ancestral home in Bangalore all his life. A retired government officer, he is deeply connected to his family's traditions, his neighbourhood, and his local temple, where he volunteers regularly. Mr. Iyer has a son, Ravi, who works as a software engineer and lives with him along with his wife and their two children. Though Ravi is devoted to his father, his work often requires him to work long hours, and he occasionally travels overseas for client visits.

**Challenges** As Mr. Iyer aged, his health declined. He has diabetes, high blood pressure, and limited mobility due to arthritis. These health issues require frequent doctor visits and medication. Additionally, with his wife's passing a few years ago, he occasionally experiences loneliness, though he remains emotionally attached to his home and reluctant to consider senior living options. The family tried hiring a part-time caregiver, but Mr. Iyer felt uncomfortable with someone outside the family in his space.

**Solutions Implemented by the Family**

1. **Home Modification for Accessibility**: Recognizing his difficulties with mobility, Ravi invested in modifying their home, adding handrails in the bathroom, widening doorways, and installing ramps to make it wheelchair-friendly. They also set up a bed on the ground floor to eliminate the need for Mr. Iyer to use stairs.
2. **Family Involvement in Care**: Ravi's wife, Sita, took on much of the caregiving responsibility, managing Mr. Iyer's medications, preparing special meals for his dietary needs, and accompanying him to the doctor. However, this added a significant workload to Sita, who also managed her children's schedules.

3. **Social Support through Neighbours and Temple**: Mr. Iyer's strong neighbourhood ties helped counteract feelings of isolation. Every evening, he walked to his neighbourhood temple with friends, where they prayed together and engaged in philosophical discussions. This routine became an essential part of his life, providing him with social interaction and emotional fulfilment.
4. **Medical Support**: Since Ravi was frequently unavailable due to work commitments, the family enlisted a nearby clinic to provide periodic check-ups for Mr. Iyer, and they registered with an emergency response service. Additionally, Ravi set up a telemedicine consultation arrangement so his father could consult doctors without needing to leave home frequently.

**Outcomes** While this arrangement posed challenges, it helped Mr. Iyer stay connected to his family and community. Though Sita and Ravi occasionally felt the strain of caregiving responsibilities, they managed to balance their roles with additional support systems. Mr. Iyer's spiritual practices and social connections also sustained him emotionally. While living at home required significant adjustment and family commitment, the solution aligned well with the family's values and Mr. Iyer's preference for staying within his familiar environment.

**Example 2: Moving to a Senior Living Community in Chennai**

**Background** Eighty-year-old Mrs. Lakshmi Ramesh lived alone in Chennai after her children moved abroad for work. Her husband passed away a decade ago, and while she used to live comfortably and independently, health concerns have made daily tasks increasingly challenging. Mrs. Ramesh has arthritis and mild memory loss, which impacts her ability to perform household chores. Though she receives frequent calls and financial support from her children, their distance and her need for regular care led the family to explore senior living communities as a practical solution.

**Challenges** Mrs. Ramesh initially resisted moving into a senior living community, fearing loss of independence, and had concerns about being in an unfamiliar environment. She worried she might not be able to continue her spiritual routines, such as her daily morning prayers, and felt apprehensive about losing contact with her social circle in her neighbourhood.

### Choosing a Senior Living Community

1. **Cultural Compatibility**: Her family found a senior living community in Chennai that catered specifically to Tamil seniors, offering a variety of cultural activities, such as bhajan sessions, religious discourse, and a small on-campus temple. This helped ease Mrs. Ramesh's worries about missing out on her religious routines.
2. **Community Structure**: The senior living community had both independent and assisted living facilities, allowing Mrs. Ramesh to maintain a sense of autonomy while also having caregivers nearby for support. This eased her transition, as she could gradually acclimate herself to needing assistance.
3. **Health and Wellness Support**: The community provided healthcare facilities, regular health check-ups, and physical therapy sessions for residents with mobility issues. The presence of an on-site nurse and doctors for emergency situations was reassuring to her children, as they no longer

worried about the immediacy of medical response in case of any emergency.
4. **Social Engagement Opportunities**: Mrs. Ramesh enjoyed meeting other residents with similar cultural backgrounds and made new friends through activities like gardening, yoga classes, and traditional cooking sessions. The community hosted seasonal festivals and religious celebrations, which allowed Mrs. Ramesh to continue her festive routines and feel a sense of continuity.

**Outcomes** Mrs. Ramesh gradually adjusted to her new surroundings and found that she enjoyed the independence afforded by the community. She appreciated the blend of companionship and independence, often inviting her children to visit when they were in the country. The professional caregiving relieved her of her daily tasks, enabling her to focus on her health and spiritual pursuits. Although it took some time for her to transition emotionally, she now feels more secure and connected within the community, appreciating the dedicated medical support and social connections. This arrangement has allowed Mrs. Ramesh's children to worry less, knowing she has reliable medical support and a vibrant social life. Although moving away from her ancestral home was difficult, the transition to a senior living community has ultimately enhanced Mrs. Ramesh's quality of life, providing both safety and engagement in her later years.

### Comparison of Outcomes in Both Examples

These two examples illustrate distinct approaches to elderly living arrangements:

- **Emotional Fulfilment and Cultural Continuity**: In both cases, cultural needs and emotional fulfilment were prioritized. Mr. Iyer's arrangement helped him maintain close family ties and stay connected to his community, while Mrs. Ramesh's senior living community integrated her cultural practices, allowing her to feel culturally fulfilled even away from her home.
- **Health and Safety Needs**: Mrs. Ramesh's senior living community provided consistent medical support, which was crucial for her safety and peace of mind, especially since her children were abroad. Mr. Iyer's family addressed his health needs with home modifications and nearby medical support, but this arrangement required more active involvement from his family members.
- **Financial and Practical Adjustments**: Each scenario entailed specific financial commitments—home modifications in Mr. Iyer's case and community fees for Mrs. Ramesh's family. Senior living communities may require a higher up-front financial commitment but provide comprehensive services, whereas living at home may be cost-effective but might require additional arrangements for healthcare and caregiving.
- **Social Interaction and Companionship**: While Mr. Iyer had his neighbourhood friends and temple group for socialization, Mrs. Ramesh's community offered organized social activities tailored to her age and cultural background, which helped her combat loneliness and build new friendships.

# Home Care vs. Professional Care: Making the Right Choice

As urbanisation and modernisation of cities continue, traditional family structures that previously shouldered the care of elders are evolving. Nuclear family models, rising professional demands, and shifting living conditions create challenges for families, leading to a rethinking of how best to support and care for elderly family members. Deciding between home care and professional care is often a significant decision that affects not only the quality of life of the elderly but also the dynamic within the family. This chapter explores home care and professional care, weighing the strengths and limitations of each. Through a focus on cultural, practical, and financial considerations, families can make an informed decision on the best option for their loved ones.

**Home Care: The Traditional Approach**

Home care has been the cornerstone of elderly care in South India, supported by a long-standing culture of intergenerational living. The concept of "Vasudhaiva Kutumbakam" (the world is one family) resonates strongly in Indian society, where elders often live with extended family and play integral roles in the household.

**Cultural and Emotional Benefits**
- **Familiarity and Comfort**: Elders often deeply connected to their homes and communities, find comfort in staying in

familiar surroundings. Emotional well-being can be significantly enhanced when they remain close to family and can participate in household activities.
- **Bond Strengthening**: In home care, family members play an active role in caregiving, allowing the elderly to feel valued and cared for by their loved ones. This also fosters stronger family bonds and a sense of purpose for the elderly, who can contribute advice and cultural guidance to younger generations.

**Logistical Challenges in Home Care**

While home care has notable benefits, the demands it places on family members, particularly the primary caregivers, can be substantial.
- **Time and Energy**: Caring for an elderly family member requires consistent attention and time. For families with young children, demanding jobs, or a lack of flexible hours, this can be difficult to manage.
- **Healthcare Needs**: Managing complex health needs such as chronic illness, dementia, or mobility issues often requires specialized knowledge. While family members may want to provide care themselves, they may lack the training or tools to handle medical issues, making effective care challenging.
- **Financial Implications**: While home care may seem more affordable at first, the cost of medical equipment, home modifications, and in some cases, the employment of part-time caregivers or nurses, can add up.

**Professional Care: The Modern Solution**

Professional elderly care is increasingly popular, especially in urban settings. Professional care includes a variety of services, from live-in nurses and specialized senior care homes to rehabilitation centres. The demand for professional care facilities in major cities like Chennai, Bengaluru, and Hyderabad reflects a shift towards practical solutions that cater to busy lifestyles.

**Types of Professional Care**
1. **Home-Based Professional Care**: Involves caregivers or nurses visiting the elderly at home to provide medical and daily living assistance, allowing them to stay in a familiar environment with a trained professional's support.
2. **Assisted Living Facilities**: These facilities provide a semi-independent living arrangement where residents receive medical supervision and daily assistance as needed. They provide a sense of community, and regular activities, and are designed to be senior-friendly.
3. **Nursing Homes and Skilled Care Facilities**: Suitable for elders who require intensive medical supervision, nursing homes provide round-the-clock medical care, tailored treatments, and physical therapy, making them ideal for individuals with chronic health issues.

**Benefits of Professional Care**
- **Access to Specialized Care**: Professional care facilities often have trained medical staff who can handle medical complexities, including chronic illnesses and rehabilitation needs. This specialized knowledge ensures that elders

receive the correct dosage of medications, timely health check-ups, and appropriate emergency responses.
- **Relief for Family Members**: Professional care can alleviate the emotional and physical demands placed on family caregivers, allowing family members to spend quality time with their loved ones without being burdened by caregiving responsibilities.
- **Structured Social Environment**: Assisted living and nursing homes offer an opportunity for elders to interact with peers, which can reduce feelings of isolation. Many facilities also provide recreational activities, therapy sessions, and community events that can enhance social engagement and cognitive health.

**Drawbacks of Professional Care**

Despite its advantages, professional care is not without drawbacks, particularly in the South Indian cultural context.
- **Cultural Misalignment**: The traditional family may struggle with guilt or social stigma associated with placing elders in professional care. The perception of "abandoning" parents or in-laws is a concern rooted deeply in cultural expectations.
- **Expense**: Professional care, particularly high-quality services, can be costly. Skilled nursing homes and long-term care facilities can pose a significant financial burden, making them inaccessible for some families without adequate insurance or savings.
- **Adjustment Difficulties**: Many elders, especially those who have spent their lives in their own homes, find it

challenging to adapt to professional care environments. Feelings of abandonment or loneliness are common, especially if family visits are infrequent.

**Key Factors to Consider in Decision-Making**

Making the choice between home care and professional care involves several considerations unique to each family's circumstances. This section outlines key factors to weigh when choosing the right care.

**Medical Requirements**

The elder's medical needs are a primary consideration. Chronic conditions that require specialized equipment, frequent medical intervention, or monitoring may necessitate professional care to ensure safety and appropriate treatment.

**Financial Capacity**

The costs associated with each type of care can vary widely. Families should evaluate expenses not only for the immediate needs but also with a long-term view, as aging often leads to progressively complex health challenges.

**Family Dynamics and Availability**

The family's structure and availability play a significant role in determining whether home care is a feasible option. Larger families with members who work from home may find it easier to provide in-home care, while smaller families or those with demanding schedules might struggle to maintain it.

**Elder's Preferences**

The elder's own wishes regarding their care environment are crucial. Some elderly people may prefer the comfort of their own home, while others may appreciate the increased socialization opportunities provided in professional care.

**Cultural Context of Families in Elderly Care**

Cultural expectations play a unique role in elderly care decisions. The tradition of caring for elders within the home is often seen as a duty and an act of reverence. However, societal norms are shifting as younger generations balance family obligations with modern careers.

**Balancing Tradition and Practicality**

Many families strive to uphold traditional values, sometimes struggling to find a balance between duty and practical realities. Family-oriented elders often feel more valued in a home care setting, where cultural rituals and family functions are part of daily life.

**Societal Perceptions and Guilt**

The stigma surrounding professional care is prevalent, with families fearing judgment from the extended community.

Professional care may be viewed by some as a "last resort," which can affect the family's decision-making process and emotional well-being. Alleviating this guilt through open conversations and understanding cultural nuances can help families make choices that are best for everyone involved.

**Government Policies and Financial Aid**

As awareness of elderly care needs grows, various government programs in these states provide support. However, many families remain unaware of these options, which could offset some costs associated with professional care or help with subsidies for home healthcare services.

**Subsidies for Medical Expenses**

Programs like the "Ayushman Bharat" scheme, which provides healthcare support to the economically disadvantaged, and state-specific schemes in Tamil Nadu and Karnataka offer financial support to elderly residents.

**Insurance Policies for Elderly Care**

Long-term health insurance plans for the elderly are available, although they may come with high premiums. Exploring these policies and understanding their coverage details can help families make more financially sound decisions.

The choice between home care and professional care is not a simple one, particularly in the culturally rich context, where family duty and respect for elders are integral to social values. Families face the challenge of balancing their cultural heritage with the practicalities of modern life, all while ensuring their elders' dignity and well-being. By considering factors such as health requirements, financial resources, family structure, and elder preferences, families can navigate this decision-making process with empathy and foresight.

In the end, there is no one-size-fits-all answer. Each family must weigh the benefits and limitations of both home care and professional care and choose the option that best aligns with their values, resources, and the needs of their elderly loved ones. Through informed decisions and compassionate support, families can honour their elders and uphold the cherished cultural values that define Indian society.

---

**Example 1: The Iyer Family — Choosing Home Care for Cultural and Emotional Reasons**

**Family Background**

The Iyer family, consisting of Mr. and Mrs. Iyer, their son Raghav, daughter-in-law Kavya, and two grandchildren, lives in Chennai. Mr. Iyer, 78, has been dealing with hypertension, diabetes, and recently, early-stage dementia. The family has a strong tradition of caregiving, with Raghav being the eldest son and the primary support for his aging parents.

**Elderly Care Decision**

After a recent hospital stay due to a minor fall, the family realized that Mr. Iyer's needs were increasing. The fall was a wake-up call for Raghav and Kavya, who wanted to ensure his safety and quality of life. Raghav's office is close to home, and Kavya is a stay-at-home mother, so they felt they could manage their time to support Mr. Iyer's care at home.

**Key Factors Considered**
1. **Cultural Beliefs**: The Iyer family places a high value on intergenerational care. Mr. Iyer had always been deeply involved in his grandchildren's lives, teaching them traditional customs and guiding them spiritually. The family felt it was their duty to provide a supportive environment where Mr. Iyer could continue being part of family activities and celebrations.
2. **Financial Feasibility**: While professional care was an option, Raghav and Kavya were concerned about the cost, especially as dementia care can become costly over time. They also realized that hiring part-time home help, like a visiting nurse for basic health monitoring and occasional physical therapy, would be a more affordable way to manage Mr. Iyer's care needs.
3. **Family Structure and Time Availability**: With Kavya at home and Raghav's work flexibility, the family decided that they could manage Mr. Iyer's care needs if they divided tasks and created a supportive home environment.

**Care Solution Implemented**

To balance care with other responsibilities, the Iyer family developed a schedule that designated specific tasks to each family member. Raghav handled all medical appointments, Kavya prepared a nutritious diet tailored to Mr. Iyer's health needs, and the grandchildren were encouraged to engage with their grandfather, learning from him and providing him with companionship.

They also hired a part-time caregiver who visited twice a week to assist with Mr. Iyer's physical therapy and mobility exercises, ensuring he maintained a safe range of movement. Additionally, they made minor modifications to their home, such as installing grab bars in the bathroom and using non-slip mats, to prevent further accidents.

**Outcome**

This setup allowed Mr. Iyer to remain at home, surrounded by family, which helped alleviate his anxiety and slow the progression of dementia symptoms. The family found a balance between tradition and practicality, enabling Mr. Iyer to age in a familiar, culturally supportive environment while ensuring he received adequate care.

## Example 2: The Menon Family — Choosing Professional Care for Specialized Support

**Family Background**

The Menon family from Bengaluru comprises Mr. and Mrs. Menon, their daughter-in-law Meera, and their son Vivek, who works in the IT industry. Mrs. Menon, 72, has advanced Parkinson's disease, which affects her mobility and daily functioning. While she lives with her family, her care needs have become increasingly demanding, especially as her condition progresses.

**Elderly Care Decision**

The family was initially committed to providing care at home, but over time, Mrs. Menon's care requirements, particularly her frequent medical episodes, grew challenging. After much deliberation, Vivek and Meera decided that moving her to a nearby specialized nursing home offering 24/7 support and Parkinson's-specific care would be in her best interest.

**Key Factors Considered**
1. **Medical Needs and Safety**: Mrs. Menon's advanced Parkinson's required constant monitoring, medication management, and daily assistance with personal care tasks like bathing, dressing, and feeding. Her frequent tremors, difficulty swallowing, and reduced mobility were making home care increasingly risky without full-time medical supervision.

2. **Financial Resources**: As Vivek and Meera were both working, they could afford the professional care costs. Additionally, they had purchased long-term health insurance for Mrs. Menon years earlier, which covered a significant portion of her nursing home expenses.
3. **Logistical Constraints**: Both Vivek and Meera worked long hours and found it difficult to provide the necessary care at home. They did not have extended family living nearby, and hiring a full-time nurse had become impractical as Mrs. Menon's care needs extended beyond home nursing capabilities.

**Care Solution Implemented**

After carefully researching options, they found a reputable assisted living facility in Bengaluru that specialized in Parkinson's care. The facility offered:
- Round-the-clock nursing and medical support.
- Physical therapy and exercises designed for Parkinson's patients.
- Social activities tailored to engage residents and reduce isolation.

The family was committed to staying involved, visiting Mrs. Menon on weekends and frequently checking in with the nursing staff to monitor her well-being.

**Outcome**

The professional care environment ensured that Mrs. Menon received specialized attention that her family could not provide at home. Her condition stabilized due to regular monitoring and therapy, and her family saw improvements in her emotional health as well. She developed friendships with other residents, which eased her transition into professional care. Although the decision was initially difficult, it proved to be beneficial for both Mrs. Menon's health and her family's peace of mind.

**Summary of Both Examples**

1. **The Iyer Family** chose **home care** due to their strong cultural values, manageable logistics, and the relatively moderate care needs of their elder. They created a hybrid approach that combined family involvement with part-time professional assistance.
2. **The Menon Family** opted for **professional care** due to the specialized medical needs of their elder and the demanding nature of their own work schedules. The professional facility provided the structure and expertise required to manage Mrs. Menon's advanced Parkinson's, relieving the family of constant worry and enabling them to focus on quality visits and emotional support.

# Technology and Aging: Innovations for Senior Care

As India experiences a demographic shift with a growing elderly population, addressing their unique healthcare, social, and lifestyle needs has become a priority. Technology has emerged as a powerful enabler in senior care, providing solutions that bridge accessibility gaps, improve quality of life, and foster independence. While the country is seeing advancements in elder care technology, there are noteworthy differences and similarities when compared to the global context, especially in Western countries where technology adoption in elder care is more established. This section explores the landscape of senior care innovations and how they compare to global developments.

**Digital Health Monitoring and Telemedicine**

Health monitoring and telemedicine technologies are making healthcare more accessible for the elderly, particularly in remote areas. Wearable health devices, such as fitness bands and smartwatches, are growing in popularity as they allow real-time monitoring of vital signs like blood pressure, heart rate, and blood sugar levels—an essential tool given the high prevalence of chronic conditions among India's elderly. Several companies are creating region-specific devices that cater to local needs and come at lower price points than many Western counterparts.

Telemedicine has also become a game-changer, allowing elderly patients to access healthcare from the safety and comfort of their homes. This is especially significant in rural areas, where medical facilities are sparse, and travel can be challenging for the elderly. Platforms like Practo and Aayu provide teleconsultation services, with user interfaces in local languages, making healthcare more inclusive for seniors unfamiliar with English. However, issues like limited internet connectivity and low digital literacy levels pose barriers that Western countries largely do not face. In many Western contexts, telemedicine is an established part of healthcare systems, offering seamless integrations with health records and highly advanced virtual diagnostics. While the country is progressing, the reach and effectiveness of telemedicine require further enhancements to match the robustness seen globally.

**Smart Home Technology for Aging in Place**

The concept of "aging in place" is central to elder care, with smart home technology enabling seniors to live independently for longer. In metropolitan cities, smart home devices like automated lighting systems, motion sensors, and voice-activated assistants are becoming more accessible. Simple yet effective innovations, such as door alarms and lighting that activates automatically, are helping elderly people navigate their homes safely. Some devices have been adapted to respond to commands in regional languages, addressing a major barrier for seniors unfamiliar with English-based technology interfaces. Globally, smart home solutions are more advanced, particularly in Western nations where AI-driven technologies provide comprehensive support. For instance, fall-detection systems in the West are increasingly equipped with artificial intelligence, enabling them to differentiate between falls and other movements. These systems often connect directly to emergency services, providing a rapid response that's largely unavailable in India, where local emergency response infrastructure is less integrated. The gradual adoption of such advanced technologies will likely depend on both technological adaptations to local contexts and infrastructure improvements.

**Digital Platforms for Social Engagement and Mental Wellness**

Isolation is a significant challenge for the elderly, particularly in urbanized sectors where traditional family structures are evolving, and seniors may live alone. Digital platforms and social media provide a lifeline for maintaining connections with family and friends. Platforms such as Seniority and Anarghyaa facilitate social interaction among seniors, allowing them to engage in virtual communities and connect with individuals facing similar life experiences.

In the global context, social engagement platforms tailored to the elderly have developed in ways that address cognitive wellness and mental health more specifically. In Western countries, virtual reality (VR) is increasingly used to help seniors combat isolation through immersive social and cultural experiences, from virtual museum tours to interactive gaming. In India, though VR adoption remains low due to high costs and infrastructure limitations, simpler mobile applications that support mental health through meditation and mindfulness are gaining popularity. These apps resonate well with India's cultural landscape, aligning with longstanding traditions of meditation and spirituality, which are particularly meaningful to the elderly population.

**Assistive Technologies for Daily Living**

Assistive devices have made a noticeable impact in elder care by enabling the elderly to perform daily activities with greater ease. Devices like walkers, rollators, adaptive utensils, and modified furniture cater to mobility and functional needs, enhancing seniors' independence and quality of life. There is also an increasing demand for affordable, senior-friendly tools that support daily living, such as easy-to-use kitchen gadgets and ergonomic chairs that aid posture and comfort.

Comparatively, assistive technology in Western countries is highly sophisticated, with access to innovations like robotic exoskeletons, sensor-based wheelchairs, and stairlifts that allow elderly individuals to maintain mobility despite physical limitations. For instance, many homes in Western nations are equipped with stairlifts for elderly residents, an innovation still relatively rare in Indian households. In addition, technologies like digital hearing aids and vision aids, such as smart glasses, are more advanced and accessible in developed countries. While the country is witnessing gradual adoption of such assistive devices, widespread implementation faces challenges, particularly around cost and availability.

**Financial Technology (Fintech) Solutions for Senior Independence**

Maintaining financial independence is crucial for the elderly, and fintech has been instrumental in simplifying money management for seniors in India. Mobile banking apps with simplified interfaces, designed with senior accessibility in mind, are empowering elderly users to manage their finances independently. Additionally, many Indian banks now offer mobile applications that include safety features to protect against fraud—a growing concern for older adults who may be less familiar with digital banking risks.

On a global scale, fintech for the elderly has progressed with features designed specifically for retirement planning and elder security. For instance, senior-friendly financial management apps in Western countries offer real-time support for managing pensions, estate planning, and health insurance in a user-friendly, streamlined way. Elder-specific fraud prevention technology, such as alerts for unusual activity, has also seen greater adoption abroad. South India is still catching up in this regard, though there are emerging tools within the Indian market that are working to provide similar safeguards.

**Challenges and Barriers in South India**

While the advancements in elder care technology are promising, there are significant challenges that hinder the widespread adoption of these innovations.

1. **Digital Literacy and Accessibility**: For many elderly individuals, navigating digital devices is a daunting task,

particularly in rural areas where digital literacy rates are lower. Government and non-profit initiatives are beginning to address this, offering digital literacy programs tailored for seniors.

2. **Cost and Affordability**: Many high-tech solutions remain financially out of reach for middle and lower-income families. Cost-effective alternatives are emerging, but they often lack the advanced features seen in Western markets, where government subsidies and healthcare systems help offset the costs of elder care technology.

3. **Cultural Resistance**: The cultural landscape can also impact technology adoption among the elderly. Many seniors are hesitant to use digital platforms, especially for healthcare, due to concerns around privacy and a preference for face-to-face interactions. This contrasts with Western nations, where elderly people are generally more open to using technology due to higher digital literacy and acceptance.

4. **Privacy and Data Security Concerns**: As digital healthcare and fintech solutions become more popular, data security is increasingly important. Elderly individuals are often wary of online data breaches, and there is a need for stronger privacy safeguards to build their confidence in using these technologies.

**Government and Institutional Support vs. Global Context**

The Indian government has taken steps to support elderly care through digital initiatives, though more robust infrastructure and support systems are seen in developed nations. Programs like the

Digital India initiative aim to improve digital access and literacy, while schemes like Ayushman Bharat have expanded healthcare access for the elderly. In contrast, countries like the United States, Japan, and several European nations have implemented extensive elder care technology policies, offering subsidies for senior-specific technologies and mandating protections for elder privacy.

Collaborations between the Indian government, non-profits, and technology providers are also crucial in creating affordable and accessible solutions. This multi-stakeholder approach helps address gaps in resources and infrastructure, which would otherwise limit technology's reach in elder care.

**Future Prospects and Innovations**

Looking ahead, the future of senior care technology is promising, with rapid advancements anticipated in several areas:

- **AI and Machine Learning for Predictive Healthcare**: AI-driven technologies can analyse health data to predict and prevent illnesses, transforming elder care by enabling early intervention. While Western countries have integrated AI in health systems, India is beginning to explore these applications, which hold great potential for the elderly.
- **Virtual Reality for Social Engagement and Cognitive Wellness**: The use of VR for cognitive and social engagement is still nascent but could provide powerful benefits, helping combat isolation and offering cognitive support.
- **Robotics and Automation**: Robotics in elder care, including companion robots, is being tested worldwide.

Although cost remains a barrier, with affordable solutions, such technologies could significantly enhance elder care in India.

Technology is reshaping elder care in India, bridging gaps in accessibility, healthcare, and social support. As the region continues to embrace innovations in elder care, challenges like digital literacy, affordability, and cultural acceptance will need to be addressed. Though the country is still evolving in comparison to the advanced elder care technologies seen globally, the future holds promise for a more inclusive and tech-enabled approach to senior care, balancing the benefits of innovation with the importance of human connection.

**Example 1: Wearable Health Monitoring Devices**

**South Indian Context:** In India, managing chronic health conditions like diabetes, hypertension, and heart disease is a significant concern among the elderly. Wearable health monitoring devices, like smartwatches and fitness trackers, have become essential for elderly people to monitor their health continuously. These devices track vital signs—such as heart rate, blood pressure, and even blood oxygen levels—and offer reminders for medication, hydration, and physical activity. Local tech startups are tailoring these devices for elderly users in India by focusing on ease of use, affordability, and language accessibility. For instance, some smartwatches are now being developed with interfaces in Tamil, Telugu, and Kannada, allowing elderly users to navigate health data in their native languages.

An example is a senior citizen named Mr. Srinivasan, a retired schoolteacher from Chennai who uses a smartwatch specifically designed for seniors. This device monitors his blood pressure, heart rate, and activity levels. Since Mr. Srinivasan has a history of hypertension, his smartwatch sends regular updates to his daughter's smartphone, alerting her if his heart rate or blood pressure deviates from normal ranges. This has allowed Mr. Srinivasan's family to feel more secure, as they can remotely monitor his health and intervene if necessary.

**Global Comparison:** Globally, wearables for elderly care are more advanced, particularly in countries like the United States and Japan. These devices often come with AI-driven predictive algorithms that alert users and caregivers not only about current health metrics but also about potential risks based on historical data. For example, some wearables in Western markets have ECG capabilities and emergency response integration, automatically contacting emergency services if a significant health event, such as a fall or irregular heartbeat, is detected. Moreover, these wearables can transmit real-time data to doctors who use it to track patients' conditions remotely, adjusting treatments as needed. The integration with formal healthcare systems in these countries provides a comprehensive monitoring system, which is still in developmental stages.

In Mr. Srinivasan's case, a similar wearable in the U.S. would likely be connected directly to his healthcare provider, with medical staff receiving updates and possibly adjusting medications based on real-time data. Although such integration is nascent, telemedicine platforms are starting to explore partnerships with wearable device manufacturers to offer similar services.

**Example 2: Smart Home Systems with Emergency Assistance**

**South Indian Context:** Smart home systems that support elderly independence are gaining traction in urban areas, especially in cities like Chennai, Bengaluru and Hyderabad. These systems are tailored to the specific safety needs of seniors living independently. For instance, motion-activated lighting, voice-activated home assistants, and emergency alert buttons are becoming popular in smart home setups for elderly residents. Mr. Narayan and Mrs. Radha, a couple in their late seventies from Bengaluru, have installed a smart home system to ensure their safety and comfort as they age in place. The system includes a motion-detecting lighting setup that lights their way if they get up at night, reducing the risk of falls. Additionally, they use a voice-activated device that allows them to make calls or request help in an emergency by simply speaking aloud, a significant benefit for elderly users who may find smartphones or tablets challenging.

Furthermore, the couple has installed emergency buttons in strategic locations throughout their home. These buttons connect directly to their son's phone, alerting him immediately if they press it in case of an emergency. While this system has provided significant peace of mind, it still requires manual intervention to activate emergency alerts, and does not directly connect to emergency medical services.

**Global Comparison:** In contrast, smart home technology in elder care is more advanced in Western countries, where AI-powered systems are equipped with predictive and proactive features. In countries like Japan and the United States, smart homes for the elderly include AI-driven emergency detection systems that recognize unusual activity patterns, such as prolonged immobility, and automatically alert emergency responders if a potential fall or medical emergency is detected. Additionally, these systems are often connected to centralized medical facilities, allowing healthcare providers to monitor seniors remotely. In a similar scenario in the U.S., Mr. Narayan and Mrs. Radha's home would likely include AI-based monitoring that could detect unusual activity and initiate an emergency response without requiring the couple to press a button. These systems use data to analyse patterns in daily routines and identify anomalies, such as not getting out of bed by a certain time or lack of movement within a usual timeframe. If such anomalies are detected, the system would automatically reach out to a designated emergency contact or medical service.

The couple's system provides essential safety features but lacks the predictive, automated intervention that Western systems offer. This gap highlights an area where elder care technology is evolving, and there is growing interest in integrating similar AI capabilities to address senior care needs proactively.

# Planning for the Future: End-of-Life Care and Decisions

End-of-life care is a critical and deeply personal aspect of aging that focuses on ensuring comfort, dignity, and respect for the elderly in their final stages of life. Planning for the future by addressing end-of-life care helps alleviate anxieties for both the elderly and their families, empowering them to make informed, compassionate choices during what can often be an emotionally charged time. For families, end-of-life decisions are influenced by culture, faith, family values, and societal expectations, and the choices made often reflect a profound respect for traditional practices. In this section, we explore the various aspects of end-of-life care planning, from understanding available care options and making medical and legal decisions to addressing emotional, spiritual, and cultural dimensions in the society.

**Understanding End-of-Life Care**

End-of-life care encompasses the medical, emotional, social, and spiritual support provided to individuals approaching the final stages of life. This type of care can begin when a person is diagnosed with a life-limiting illness or when it becomes evident that they may not recover from a serious health condition. End-of-life care options often include:
- **Palliative Care**: This focuses on providing relief from the symptoms, pain, and stress of a serious illness. Palliative

care can begin at any stage of a life-limiting illness and often works alongside curative treatments.
- **Hospice Care**: Hospice care is a form of palliative care provided when curative treatment is no longer pursued, typically when the individual is estimated to have six months or less to live. Hospice care prioritizes comfort, symptom management, and emotional support, allowing the elderly to spend their remaining time with quality and dignity.
- **Home-Based End-of-Life Care**: Many families prefer to keep their elders at home during their final stages of life, both for emotional closeness and because it aligns with cultural values of caring for elders within the family unit.

## Communicating with Family and Care Providers

Effective communication among the elderly, family members, and healthcare providers is crucial to ensuring that end-of-life care reflects the wishes and values of the person receiving care. This can be challenging, as discussions about death and dying are often considered taboo or uncomfortable in Indian culture. However, fostering open dialogue can:
- Alleviate fear and anxiety for the elderly by addressing their concerns directly.
- Help family members understand and respect the elder's wishes for care, minimizing conflicts or confusion.
- Allow healthcare providers to create a care plan that is consistent with the individual's values and preferences.

**Legal and Medical Planning for End-of-Life Care**

Legal and medical planning helps prepare for end-of-life care decisions in advance, ensuring that the elderly person's preferences are followed. Common tools include:

- **Advance Directives**: An advance directive is a legal document that allows an individual to outline their healthcare preferences in case they become unable to make decisions. It can include instructions on preferred treatments, resuscitation preferences, and the use of life-support machines.
- **Living Will**: A living will provides instructions for specific medical interventions a person would or would not like to receive if they are terminally ill or incapacitated. This can be essential for reducing ambiguity during emergencies.
- **Power of Attorney (POA)**: It is common for families to appoint a trusted family member to manage healthcare or financial decisions on behalf of an elderly relative. The POA can be a Healthcare POA, allowing the designated person to make medical decisions, or a Financial POA, allowing them to manage finances.

In Indian families, choosing a family member for POA is often based on trust, understanding of the elderly person's wishes, and availability. Clear communication about the responsibilities involved is important to avoid family misunderstandings.

**Emotional and Psychological Support for the Elderly and Families**

The emotional journey of end-of-life care involves complex feelings of fear, sadness, guilt, and acceptance, affecting both the elderly and their loved ones. Families can support their elders emotionally by:

- **Offering Consistent Reassurance and Companionship**: Being present and providing companionship can alleviate loneliness and fear, enhancing emotional well-being.
- **Professional Counselling and Support Groups**: Indian society is gradually opening up to the idea of professional mental health services. Engaging a counsellor can help the elderly and family members cope with feelings of loss, grief, and anticipatory grief.
- **Encouraging Expressions of Unresolved Feelings**: In a traditional society where elders may feel pressured to "hold back" their worries, creating a space for them to express their fears and wishes can be healing.
- **Providing Grief Counselling for Families**: Post-bereavement support for family members can help them process the loss and move forward in a healthy way, respecting the memory of their loved one.

**The Role of Spirituality and Religious Practices**

In traditional families, spirituality and religious practices often play a pivotal role in end-of-life care. For many, spiritual beliefs offer comfort and meaning, providing a framework for understanding mortality. Some ways in which spirituality influences end-of-life care include:

- **Rituals and Prayers**: Most Indians find solace in performing traditional rituals and prayers, believing that these actions support the soul's journey. Family members may chant or perform poojas (ritualistic worship) to help their loved one find peace.
- **Seeking Guidance from Religious Leaders**: Many families consult with priests or religious leaders who provide insights on ethical or moral dilemmas surrounding end-of-life care. Such guidance can offer comfort and clarity, especially for decisions like life-support or organ donation.
- **Encouraging Spiritual Practices**: Some elderly individuals find peace in meditation, chanting, or reading religious texts, and families can support them by facilitating these practices, even if it means adjusting care routines.

**Financial Planning for End-of-Life Care**

Financial preparedness can relieve some of the burdens associated with end-of-life care and ensure that necessary resources are available for treatment and support. In the current context, financial planning may include:

- **Insurance Policies**: Health insurance can cover some costs of end-of-life care, though families should review their policies for specific details on coverage for palliative or hospice care.
- **Setting Up a Fund for Care Costs**: In many households, families contribute collectively to cover the costs of end-

of-life care. Having a designated fund can reduce stress and prevent financial strain during critical times.
- **Considering Long-Term Care Plans**: With life expectancy rising, some families invest in long-term care plans that cover future care needs, including home nursing, palliative care, and support for chronic illnesses.
- **Addressing Inheritance and Property Matters**: While discussing inheritance and property allocation can be sensitive, clear documentation helps prevent conflicts. Legal support may be sought to draft wills, trust deeds, or family agreements that align with the elderly person's wishes.

**Home Care vs. Institutional Care Decisions**

Deciding between home care and institutional care can be a challenging aspect of end-of-life planning, influenced by the individual's health, family capacity, and preferences. In current day society, the preference is often for home care, allowing elders to remain in a familiar environment. However, institutional care can be beneficial if the elderly require round-the-clock medical attention. Key considerations include:
- **Quality of Life**: Home care provides a sense of comfort and continuity. However, if an individual requires intensive medical support, a hospital or palliative care centre may offer better quality of life through specialized care.
- **Availability of Family Members**: In situations where family members cannot provide adequate care, hiring trained caregivers or considering a reputable hospice may be appropriate.

- **Costs**: Institutional care can be expensive, and financial resources may impact the decision. Home care, while often less costly, may still require resources for modifications, equipment, and caregiver support.

**Dying with Dignity: Euthanasia and End-of-Life Ethics**

Discussions around euthanasia and the "right to die" are sensitive, and perspectives vary widely in the society. While euthanasia is currently illegal in India, the debate on passive euthanasia—allowing a person to die by withholding life-support treatments—has gained attention, especially for patients in extreme pain or vegetative states.

Ethical decisions surrounding end-of-life care often weigh individual wishes against religious, societal, and familial values. Passive euthanasia, though controversial, is sometimes viewed as a way to ensure a dignified passing, free from prolonged suffering. Families are encouraged to consult medical professionals, religious leaders, and legal advisors to navigate these complex decisions.

**Documenting and Reviewing End-of-Life Care Plans**

Creating a comprehensive end-of-life care plan is a dynamic process that may need regular review as circumstances change. A documented plan can be invaluable for ensuring that the individual's wishes are honoured, even if they lose the ability to communicate them. Key steps include:
- **Reviewing Plans Periodically**: Circumstances, health conditions, and family dynamics may change over time, so

reviewing care plans annually ensures they remain relevant.
- **Engaging with Family Members**: Discussing end-of-life care decisions openly, especially with those directly involved, reduces the likelihood of confusion or conflict.
- **Maintaining Accessible Records**: Keeping documents like advance directives, medical reports, and the will in an accessible place ensures that family members have the information they need during critical moments.

End-of-life care and planning for the future are deeply personal yet necessary steps in aging. In Indian families, decisions around end-of-life care are often made collectively, balancing the elderly individual's wishes with cultural expectations and practical realities.

---

**Example 1: Balancing Family Expectations and an Elder's Wishes**

**Scenario**: Mrs. Lakshmi, a 78-year-old retired teacher from Chennai, has been diagnosed with terminal cancer. Her health is declining rapidly, and her pain requires constant management. She has been living with her son, daughter-in-law, and two grandchildren. Mrs. Lakshmi has expressed a wish to receive palliative care at home, preferring to spend her final days in a familiar environment rather than in a hospital. She also made it clear that she does not want aggressive treatments like chemotherapy at this stage, desiring a peaceful, pain-managed transition.

**Challenge**: Mrs. Lakshmi's son, however, feels uncomfortable with the idea of her remaining at home as her condition worsens. He believes she might be better cared for in a hospital, where emergency medical support is available at all times. As the primary breadwinner, he feels a responsibility to provide the "best" medical support, even if it means institutional care. He also struggles with the emotional burden of "letting go" and fears the family will be judged if she does not receive hospital care.

**Resolution**: The family holds a meeting with Mrs. Lakshmi's palliative care doctor to openly discuss her wishes, explain the benefits of home palliative care, and address her son's concerns. The doctor reassures the family that Mrs. Lakshmi's symptoms can be managed at home with support from a trained nurse and pain management medications, allowing her to remain comfortable. With this professional guidance, Mrs. Lakshmi's son feels more confident about fulfilling her wishes, and the family creates a plan for rotating caregiving duties, ensuring Mrs. Lakshmi can remain at home with the care she needs.

**Key Takeaway**: This example underscores the importance of open family communication and professional support in end-of-life decision-making. It highlights the balance between respecting the elder's wishes and managing family members' emotions and expectations.

**Example 2: Legal Planning and the Role of Advance Directives**

**Scenario**: Mr. Rajan, an 82-year-old businessman from Bengaluru, has been experiencing serious complications due to advanced-stage kidney disease. Aware of his deteriorating health, Mr. Rajan decides to take proactive steps to outline his end-of-life preferences, including appointing his elder daughter, Meena, as his healthcare power of attorney (POA). He also creates an advance directive, specifying that he does not want to be placed on life support or undergo aggressive treatments if his prognosis becomes terminal.

**Challenge**: When Mr. Rajan experiences a sudden health crisis and is admitted to the hospital, his younger daughter, Priya, who was unaware of the advance directive, insists on aggressive treatments, including intubation and ventilator support, as she believes these interventions could extend his life. Priya is emotionally unprepared for the situation and feels strongly that "everything possible" should be done. The family faces a dilemma, torn between honouring Mr. Rajan's advance directive and respecting Priya's wishes.

**Resolution**: The hospital staff meets with the family to review Mr. Rajan's advance directive and explain the importance of honouring his documented preferences. The medical team provides information on Mr. Rajan's condition, explaining how aggressive interventions may cause more suffering without significantly improving his quality of life. With support from healthcare professionals, Priya eventually comes to terms with her father's wishes. She agrees to follow the advance directive, allowing Mr. Rajan to pass peacefully and with dignity, as he had intended.

**Key Takeaway**: This example demonstrates how advance directives and legal tools, like a healthcare power of attorney, can guide families through difficult decisions and help prevent conflict by clearly stating the elder's wishes in advance.

# Part 6

# Future of Elder Care in South India

# The Future of Elderly Care in Urban South India

As urban India continues to evolve, the future of elderly care faces both promising developments and considerable challenges. With shifting demographics, changing family structures, and a rapidly advancing technological landscape, the ways we approach aging are undergoing significant transformations. This section explores key aspects likely to shape the future of elderly care in urban India, focusing on emerging trends in caregiving, innovative solutions, healthcare advancements, socio-economic dynamics, and the cultural values that remain integral to elder care in this region.

**Demographic Shifts and the Increasing Elderly Population**

The rapid growth of the elderly population is one of the most significant factors influencing the future of elderly care in South India. According to recent data, India's elderly population is projected to reach over 194 million by 2031, with South India hosting a considerable share due to factors like better healthcare and higher life expectancy rates. Urban areas, particularly in South Indian metros like Bengaluru, Chennai, Hyderabad, and Kochi, are experiencing this demographic shift more acutely. As the demand for senior-specific resources rises, it will likely strain existing healthcare and social support systems. Policymakers, urban planners, and private sector stakeholders will need to invest in sustainable solutions for elderly housing, healthcare, and community engagement, ensuring that urban infrastructure evolves to meet these growing needs.

**Changing Family Structures and Caregiving Models**

Traditionally, elderly care has been a familial responsibility, with family members living in close proximity and sharing caregiving duties. However, urbanization and the outmigration of younger generations for education and employment have led to more nuclear family setups, reducing the availability of family caregivers. In the future, elderly care in cities will likely shift to more formalized models, such as professional home care services and assisted living communities, which can offer tailored support for seniors.

At the same time, multigenerational households are likely to evolve to accommodate elderly members better, with an emphasis on fostering independence while providing support. The emergence of professional caregivers, especially those trained to meet the specific needs of elderly, will become more prominent, requiring increased investment in caregiving training programs and certifications. Furthermore, partnerships between families and care providers may emerge as families seek ways to stay involved in their elders' care despite physical distance.

**Innovations in Healthcare and Technology for Elderly Care**

Technology is poised to play a transformative role in elderly care in urban India. The growth of telemedicine, wearable health devices, and remote monitoring systems are already beginning to enhance healthcare access for the elderly, a trend likely to expand in the future. Through telemedicine, seniors in urban areas can consult specialists without traveling, reducing physical strain and saving time. Remote monitoring devices that track vital health metrics and detect emergencies, such as falls, are improving the quality of care and enabling seniors to remain independent.

Artificial Intelligence (AI) and Internet of Things (IoT) applications are set to revolutionize elderly care further by enabling predictive analytics that could prevent health crises before they occur. In metropolitan cities, where traffic and transportation challenges can affect healthcare access, these technologies have immense potential. Moreover, smartphone applications and digital platforms tailored for elderly users will facilitate easy access to services ranging from healthcare and grocery delivery to community interactions and spiritual engagements, ensuring that seniors stay connected and supported.

**Financial Planning and Accessibility to Elderly Care Services**

Financial stability is a cornerstone of quality elderly care, yet many seniors face challenges due to limited pension coverage or inadequate retirement savings. As a result, the future of elderly care will likely involve greater emphasis on financial planning tools and resources. Financial literacy programs for both the elderly and their families will be essential to help them manage healthcare costs, secure insurance coverage, and invest in long-term care solutions.

Additionally, the rising costs of professional care services and elder-specific housing are anticipated to make financial planning a critical aspect of elder care. Private and public institutions could develop innovative financing options, such as long-term care insurance and reverse mortgage options tailored to seniors. These financial solutions can empower elderly individuals to access necessary care without overburdening their families.

**Senior-Friendly Urban Infrastructure and Inclusive Design**

As India urbanizes, there will be an increasing demand for senior-friendly public spaces and infrastructure. Accessibility in public spaces, such as markets, temples, parks, and community centres, will become a priority. Cities may adopt urban planning models that promote "aging in place," allowing elderly individuals to continue residing in their familiar environments with accessible amenities.

Urban architecture will likely shift towards age-inclusive designs, incorporating features like ramps, handrails, wider walkways, and resting spots, ensuring safe and convenient mobility for seniors. Transportation systems, including public buses, metros, and ride-sharing platforms, will also adapt to accommodate elderly passengers, making transit easier and more comfortable. In the future, these changes could transform urban areas in South India into hubs of age-inclusive living, reducing isolation and promoting independence among elderly residents.

## Emergence of Specialized Elderly Housing Communities

The concept of specialized senior living communities is gaining traction in South India, and this trend is expected to accelerate. These communities offer facilities tailored to the unique needs of seniors, such as healthcare services, recreational facilities, wellness programs, and social engagement activities. Future developments may see more such communities emerge, providing a balance of comfort, safety, and companionship.

As this sector grows, senior living communities may evolve to offer varying levels of care, from independent living to assisted living and memory care units, catering to a broad spectrum of physical and cognitive needs. Indian cultural values can be incorporated into these communities, ensuring that they offer familiar customs, traditions, and dietary practices, which are particularly important for seniors. Such initiatives will not only meet the healthcare needs of elderly residents but also promote social interaction and a sense of belonging.

## Mental Health and Social Inclusion in Elderly Care

Loneliness, social isolation, and mental health issues are critical challenges that elderly individuals face, particularly in urban settings. The future of elderly care will need to address mental well-being as much as physical health. As awareness about mental health continues to grow, there will likely be more resources dedicated to tackling issues such as depression, anxiety, and cognitive decline among the elderly.

Community-based programs that foster intergenerational connections, encourage participation in cultural activities, and promote spiritual and religious engagement will be vital. Faith-based organizations, a core component of the society, could play a significant role in promoting mental well-being by organizing community events, meditation programs, and cultural gatherings. Furthermore, online platforms and apps that connect seniors with their families, caregivers, and peer groups will also help alleviate social isolation and provide emotional support.

**Role of Government Policies and Initiatives**

The Indian government has implemented several schemes aimed at improving elderly welfare, including the National Programme for Health Care of the Elderly (NPHCE) and the Indira Gandhi National Old Age Pension Scheme (IGNOAPS). In the future, more region-specific policies and initiatives will likely emerge to cater to the urban elderly. As the elderly population grows, state governments could introduce tax benefits, healthcare subsidies, and affordable housing schemes designed for seniors, further easing the financial burden on both seniors and their families.

Public-private partnerships could also play an essential role in this domain. Collaboration between government bodies, healthcare providers, and senior care organizations can create comprehensive support frameworks that extend beyond basic medical care, encompassing social, emotional, and economic needs. By encouraging investment in elder care, the government can also foster innovation in senior-friendly housing and elder-specific healthcare services, building a strong foundation for future care models.

## Cultural Adaptations in Elderly Care

South India has a rich cultural heritage, and integrating cultural values into elderly care will remain a priority. The future of elderly care in urban India will likely see a harmonious blend of traditional values with modern caregiving practices. Family involvement, even in professional care settings, will continue to be emphasized, with family members often staying involved in decision-making processes.

Cultural practices, including dietary habits, festival celebrations, and religious observances, will shape the lifestyle within elderly care facilities and senior living communities. Customized care approaches that honour these cultural elements will enhance the quality of life for seniors, helping them maintain a connection to their roots while receiving the support they need.

## The Need for a Skilled Workforce in Elderly Care

With a growing elderly population, there will be an increased demand for trained professionals in geriatric care, including nurses, caregivers, physical therapists, and social workers. Building a skilled workforce will require investments in training programs that focus on geriatric care and understand the specific needs of the elders. The future will see more vocational courses and certifications tailored to elder care, ensuring that caregivers have the requisite skills to address the physical and emotional needs of seniors.

Additionally, professionalization in elderly care services will be essential, as families in urban areas increasingly rely on paid caregivers. Care providers who are not only well-trained in healthcare but also sensitive to cultural norms will become the cornerstone of elderly care in urban South India, offering services that are both efficient and empathetic.

The future of elderly care in urban society will be shaped by a delicate balance of modern advancements and traditional values. As demographic shifts accelerate and urbanization continues, adapting to the changing needs of the elderly population will require collaboration among government agencies, private sectors, and communities. By fostering inclusivity, encouraging financial planning, advancing technological solutions, and maintaining cultural sensitivities, urban South India can create an environment where seniors live with dignity, comfort, and a sense of belonging. The journey forward calls for innovative thinking, compassionate approaches, and a commitment to providing comprehensive support for our elderly, ensuring they age gracefully and remain integral members of our society.

# Afterword

The journey of *SUNRISE YEARS* has been one of introspection, exploration, and dedication to a cause that transcends mere duty—it is rooted in the deep respect and compassion our culture holds for the elderly. As I reflect on the themes explored within these pages, I am reminded that senior care is not simply a social responsibility but a moral and emotional commitment to ensuring that our elders live with dignity, fulfilment, and the warmth of community support.

The South Indian context brings with it unique challenges and opportunities. Our heritage is rich with values of respect for age and wisdom, yet our society is evolving rapidly. The influence of urbanization, technological advancement, and shifting family dynamics continually reshapes how we engage with our elderly. Throughout this book, I've endeavoured to balance these perspectives, offering a comprehensive framework for elder care that honours tradition while embracing the future.

I hope this book serves as a roadmap for caregivers, families, and senior care professionals to navigate the complexities of elder care with clarity and compassion. The discussions around home care versus professional care, the role of spirituality, and the nuances of financial and legal planning reflect a deep understanding of the decisions faced by South Indian families today. As we look forward, I believe the future of elder care in urban South India lies in an integrated approach—one that leverages community support, embraces innovative solutions, and respects each individual's unique needs and wishes.

In closing, *SUNRISE YEARS* is more than a book; it is an invitation to all readers to consider their role in shaping a future where our elderly are cherished, empowered, and provided for in every way. The "sunrise years" are a time of reflection, wisdom, and often renewed purpose, both for the elderly and for those who care for them. Let us all, together, commit to making these years as bright, dignified, and fulfilling as possible.

**With gratitude and hope,**
*Ashwin Kumar Iyer*

www.ingramcontent.com/pod-product-compliance
Lightning Source LLC
LaVergne TN
LVHW061609070526
838199LV00078B/7220